M

THE TATTOO MURDERS

After a tempestuous struggle, the visitor tossed the pillow aside. Life had ceased. The killer turned Vera over on her face and ripped the satin jacket of her pyjamas. Upon her back was a tattooed name — 'MARY'. Dispassionately, the intruder wrote the name down, returned to the window and disappeared. 'Mary', 'Ian', 'Lil'. Three rather ordinary names. But when they are each found tattooed on the backs of three murder victims, they are stepping-stones on a murder trail that baffles Scotland Yard.

JOHN RUSSELL FEARN

THE TATTOO MURDERS

Complete and Unabridged

LINFORD
Leicester

First published in 1949
under the title 'Murder's A Must'

First Linford Edition
published 2005

British Library CIP Data

Fearn, John Russell, *1908 – 1960*
    The tattoo murders.—Large print ed.—
Linford mystery library
    1. Murder—Investigation—Great Britain—
Fiction 2. Serial murders—Great Britain—
Fiction 3. Detective and mystery stories
    4. Large type books
    I. Title
    823.9'12 [F]

ISBN 1–84395–740–X

Published by
F. A. Thorpe (Publishing)
Anstey, Leicestershire

Set by Words & Graphics Ltd.
Anstey, Leicestershire
Printed and bound in Great Britain by
T. J. International Ltd., Padstow, Cornwall

This book is printed on acid-free paper

1

The highbrows who condescended to visit Madame Luchaire's Gown Salon were not aware that the proprietress, a tall, slinky woman in form-fitting black silk with suspiciously blonde hair, had actually been christened Vera Bradmore. They assumed she was French, and for that reason alone her creations just had to be just too-too . . .

To her patrons, which included those who paid as well as the other variety, Vera Bradmore was definitely 'charmeeing,' with her slightly phony accent and shoulder twitching; but to her staff and immediate associates she was plain 'Vera,' or even 'Old Girl Bradmore,' and the possessor of the devil's own temper.

On this particular afternoon in late spring Vera was even more bad-tempered than usual. Things had gone wrong in the morning and progressively deteriorated throughout the day. First it had been the mistake in the dressmaking department — which had cost her one of her best customers; then through minor trifles tragedy had reached its culminating point this afternoon with her head saleswoman accidentally ripping a priceless creation with her too vigorous hands. And in front of Dowager Lady Brandisbrook, too.

In a word, Vera was fuming. She sat now at her five-acre walnut desk in the private office, drumming on its top with scarlet-painted fingernails. She was waiting for the head saleswoman, waiting to unleash her invective. This gathering storm made Vera's heavily made-up face rather pinker than usual and lent an added brightness to her clear blue eyes. She was a good-looking woman, with a straight nose and firm mouth. Only her too pointed chin betrayed her quick, impulsive anger. An older woman might have controlled herself more firmly. At twenty-eight Vera believed in controlling other people — not herself.

The polished walnut door opened silently before a light preliminary knock and the head saleswoman, Claire Wilton, came in gracefully. An ex-mannequin, she still walked like one, advancing to the desk as if balancing the *Encyclopedia Britannica* on her head.

'You sent for me, Miss Bradmore?'

'Yes, I certainly did!' Vera Bradmore glared up at her from the desk. 'It won't take long to say what I have to say, either. You're discharged!'

Claire Wilton's expression changed slightly. She had a sallow complexion, sultry dark eyes, and exuded the aroma of roses in full bloom.

'May I ask . . . why?' she enquired frigidly.

'Why? *Why?*' Vera Bradmore waved a hand in the air in her best pseudo-French style. 'Great heavens, isn't it obvious? You ruined that Les Montaine creation this afternoon, and with Lady Brandisbrook looking on! In case you're not aware of it, she told me all about it . . . and she was so revolted by your clumsiness she vowed never to patronize my salon again! This morning I lost the Countess Barinski, and now you have lost me her Ladyship! It's time you went, Miss Wilton!'

'I hardly consider that one slight mistake after five years' impeccable service warrants my discharge!' Claire Wilton retorted.

'You are in no position to consider anything!' Vera snapped. 'Get out! I can't afford to have bunglers around me. I've built up this business from nothing, and I don't intend that incompetents should drag it down.'

'Built it up from nothing . . . ' Claire Wilton seemed to reflect, smiling sourly. 'Yes, that's very true, I suppose. You came from the gutter, didn't you?'

Vera's blue eyes flashed. 'How dare you?'

'I dare quite easily since I'm discharged. I'll be glad to go, really.' Polish was falling from the head saleswoman like paint under a blowlamp. 'I've always hated the sight of you ever since I came into the place. Your whole confounded dress business is built on deception. Everybody on the staff knows your French stuff is a pose — but what everybody does not know is that you originated in the East End, the London gutter, and that you've only got as far as you have by browbeating and bullying your way. You're cheap, 'Madame Luchaire' — disgustingly cheap!'

Vera Bradmore sat and stared, unable to think of an appropriate reply.

'I made a point of finding it all out,' Claire Wilton said. 'Not that it does me any good, except that it prepared me in advance for what's happening now. No woman of breeding would fire her head saleswoman for the slight mistake I made with that dress. You just want to feel your miserable little bit of power, don't you?'

'Get out of here!' Vera said, showing her white teeth. 'Go on — get out!'

'With pleasure . . . ' Claire Wilton's eyes were cold. 'But I'm not going with good grace, Miss Bradmore. You haven't heard the last of this, believe me!'

She swung to the door, departed, and slammed the door behind her. Vera snapped the intercom switch on her desk, and the head cashier answered.

'Miss Wilton will be applying for her salary to date in a moment or two. See she gets it.'

'Very good, Miss Bradmore.'

Vera pressed another switch and summoned the female house detective who kept a watch on the valuables in the salon. She arrived in a moment, five-feet-ten of well-upholstered womanhood, yet dressed in a manner which was not a give-away as to her occupation.

'Yes, Miss Bradmore?' the woman asked and stood waiting with the air of a wardress.

'Miss Wilton is leaving us,' Vera said briefly. 'I have had reason to discharge her. Before departing, she was grossly insulting and vowed she would get even with me, or some such threat. I want you to keep a special eye open for my welfare. Employees nurse imagined grudges sometimes.'

The Amazon gave a grim, understanding smile.

'I understand perfectly, Miss Bradmore. You can rely on me. That woman won't cause you any trouble.'

'Thanks. That's all.'

The woman left with firm tread, and for a while Vera sat at her desk, frowning. She would not admit it for a moment, not even to herself, but she now almost regretted having been so tough about things. Claire Wiltons did not grow on trees; to find a new head saleswoman with her skill would be difficult. But tearing that gown! And in front of her Ladyship! Vera became warm again at the thought ... Finally she flicked the intercom switch once more.

'Miss Chantry?' she enquired, naming her secretary. 'See an advertisement goes in tonight's paper for a head saleswoman. Interviews from tomorrow onwards. If anything more is needed hold it until tomorrow. I've an appointment.'

'Yes, Miss Bradmore.'

Vera switched off, took her hat and overcoat from the highly polished wardrobe in the corner, and slipped them on. She considered herself in the full-length mirror and was quite satisfied by what she saw. There could certainly be no cause for complaint on the part of her fiancé, anyway.

She had her chauffeur drive her to the appointed meeting place — Vantry's Restaurant in the city — and there dismissed him. As it chimed six from the nearby church clock, Derek Cantrill came into view — tall, elegant, bowler-hatted, a crooked umbrella over his arm, and wearing a suit that said stocks-and-shares.

'Right on time, my dear,' he murmured, as he came up with bowler raised from sand-colored hair. 'I — '

'Three minutes late,' Vera reproved.

'But, my dear, the clock has only just finished striking! Honestly, Vera, I do think there are times when you try to be awkward just for the sake of it.'

Since this was definitely true, Vera did not pursue the subject. She motioned to the restaurant, and Derek Cantrill set the revolving door on the move for her and then followed her into the warm, softly-lighted interior. There were not many diners present and to select a corner table was simple.

'I'm hungry,' Vera said bluntly as the waiter hovered.

Derek Cantrill affected not to notice a distinct lack of breeding in Vera's observation and gave his order. Then he sat back and considered Vera thoughtfully.

She gazed back at him with the direct stare she had and which, more than anything else, betrayed her dubious upbringing.

'Well, anything wrong?' she asked at last.

Derek Cantrill reflected. He was a tall, dandified young man with artistic tastes, forced to follow stocks and shares because his artistry expended more money than it gained.

'I think,' he said, with a half smile, 'that everything is!'

Vera laughed shortly. 'Whatever your troubles are, Derek, they can't be any worse than what I have had to tolerate today! Ever since I got up this morning nothing has been right.'

He sighed. 'Which does not make it any easier for me to say what I'm thinking. Briefly . . . ' He looked down at his immaculate hands on the table edge. 'Briefly, my dear, I think we should bring this farce to an end.'

Vera started and then sat for a moment staring at him.

'Farce? What farce?'

'Our association. We're not cut out for each other, you know. I mean . . . our tastes are different. I thought when I first met you at your salon, when my sister wanted my opinion on that new dress she was buying, that we had a great deal in common. I suppose I fell for your French pose and frothy manners. In the weeks that have passed since, which we have spent in close association, I have realized that there are . . . differences.'

'What you mean is, you don't think I'm good enough for you?' Vera snapped, coloring under the rouge.

'I didn't say that. I never would to a lady.'

'You don't think I am a lady! You've as good as said so! You have the high-flown notion that you're high up and I'm low down! That's it, isn't it?'

'Honestly, Vera, I'm convinced that for both our sakes it would be better to break everything off — '

Derek stopped as he realized the waiter had arrived. Inscrutable in his expression, though he must have heard most of the conversation, he served the meal and then retired. Vera sat with her lips tight, a vicious glint in her blue eyes.

'This about finishes everything!' she said at last. 'I've been told once before today that I'm cheap, and now you start off on the same tack! You don't think I'm going to stand for it, do you?'

'It's a matter of viewpoint,' Derek said, thinking. 'Since it's quite obvious no possible harmony could come of us being married, why should we keep up the pretense?'

'You started this business, not me!' Vera nearly shouted, jumping to her feet. 'Don't think you can treat me like dirt, Derek, and get away with it. Look! See that!' She held out her left hand with the big diamond engagement ring. 'That says I am engaged to you, and you'll either stand by it or I'll drag you into court for breach of promise. I've letters from you; I've everything! I could win! I could make you marry me — or else make your name smell so much that no other girl would!'

Derek gazed up at her fixedly, secretly amazed at the dynamite he had touched off. He hovered over some kind of

11

protest, but Vera did not give him the time to utter it.

'Think it over,' she said briefly. 'When you have better sense, give me a ring on the phone. You entered into a bargain with me, Derek — and you're going to stick to it.'

With that she turned, her meal ignored, and swept out of the café. Derek stared towards the revolving doors as they slowed down to a stop, then catching the eye of the distant waiter who was trying to look disinterested, he turned back to the table. He did not eat; he sat thinking.

In the meantime, since she had dismissed her car, Vera had to descend to the plebeian practice of taking a taxi to Kensington. Here she had her luxurious service flat on the fourth floor. Entering it, she snapped on the lights, flung down her hat and coat into a chair, and spent nearly five minutes pacing angrily up and down. Derek's decision to break things off, coming on top of all the other incidents during the day, had about brought her to the breaking point. She felt inclined to violence as her uncontrollable temper got the upper hand, then realizing violence might endanger the valuable furniture and artworks in the flat, she had got a hold over herself.

'See if I care!' she breathed, staring venomously at her reflection in the mirror as she lighted a cigarette. 'He'll not get away with it! By heaven, he won't!'

She swung away angrily and went into the small kitchenette. She had discovered she was still hungry. After she had eaten and drunk some coffee, she had changed into a mood of cold, stolid bitterness against the world in general. Finally, towards ten o'clock, she retired to bed — not to sleep, but to lie and think how she would deal with Derek if he dared to carry things as far as a court.

She lay propped up in the pillows, supremely comfortable physically if not mentally. The only light came from the bedside lamp that cast a circle of brilliance on the satin eiderdown, and a lesser, diffused cone on the cream colored ceiling. The remainder of the room was in deepest shadow.

After a while she became aware of faint sounds. At first she assumed the tenants in the flat above were responsible — then to her astonishment she realized the noise was coming from the heavily curtained window, She was still trying to analyze things and make up her mind what she would do when a draught of cold air momentarily disturbed the window drapes. A second later they parted and closed again.

Blankly, Vera half lay staring at the intruder. The figure came forward silently, face shadowed by the brim of a hat.

'What on — Who on earth are you?' Vera gasped, aware that her heart was thumping painfully.

The visitor halted at the bedside and smiled. It was not a smile of welcome, but cold and relentless.

'You have two sisters,' the intruder said quietly. 'You and your two sisters are triplets.'

'Yes . . . Yes, that's right,' Vera admitted hurriedly, and wished desperately that she had a revolver.

'Very well then. Where are they?'

'Why should I tell you that?' Vera demanded, hers eyes glinting.

'You know perfectly well why. Unless you tell me where they are, it will be the worse for you.'

'I — I — ' Vera hesitated, realizing the hands of the intruder were strong. She herself had never possessed very great physical strength. At heart nothing was more valuable to her than her own well-being. So perhaps she had better talk.

'They're married,' she said haltingly. 'Elsie is now Mrs. Jackson — '

'Living where?'

'Just outside the City. 47 Kendal Rise, Surbiton.'

The intruder quickly made a note on a small pocket pad. 'And Janice? Where is she?'

'She's Mrs. Mottram now. Living at The Larches, Crescent Avenue, Maida Vale.'

'Gone up in the world, both of them, like you, eh?' There was a low laugh from the shadows. 'Since you know perfectly well why I want them, I'm not going to waste time explaining'

There was silence for a moment. Vera, filled with the imminent fear of danger, lay staring with wide eyes.

'What — what do you intend doing with me?' she asked finally.

'Making sure you don't talk. I might find it awkward if you decided to inform the police of what has gone on here tonight.'

'Why don't you come out of the shadows so that I can see you properly?' Vera demanded hoarsely. 'All I can see are your hands — but I know your voice! I've heard it many a time — even though I think you're trying to disguise it now! Why don't you — ?'

Vera could not speak any further. With a lithe movement, the visitor suddenly stepped forward and for an instant Vera had the chance to look at the face — then the view was blotted out as one of the many pillows was brought down tightly upon her.

She squirmed and struggled violently as she felt herself smothering in the folds;

but the harder she fought the tighter the suffocating wad crushed down upon her.

Finally, after a tempestuous struggle, the visitor straightened up, breathing hard, and tossed the pillow on one side. An investigation of Vera's pulse proved that life had ceased. She lay motionless, her blue eyes glazing, a purplish tinge in her face from the slow stifling she had received.

Without any ceremony the killer turned Vera over onto her face and with one strong hand ripped the satin jacket of her pyjamas straight down from the collar, the two halves folding gently to each side. The back of the dead woman lay, clearly revealed in the lamplight. Low down upon it, perhaps three inches below the level of the shoulder-blades, was a tattooed name — 'MARY.'

No more than that, and apparently no effort had ever been made to eradicate the imprint. Dispassionately the intruder wrote the name down in the scratchpad, then with hardly a sound, returned to the window and disappeared.

2

The chambermaid for the service flats, whose duty it was to bring morning tea to those tenants who desired it, was the first person to find Vera's corpse. She took one long, baffled look at the sprawled body, with the name 'Mary' clearly tattooed upon the back, and then fled — the tray and tea so firmly glued in her hands as she moved she did not spill a drop.

The proprietor of the flats came next, eased his collar, and swallowed hard; then gave orders for the room to be locked and no information to escape to the other tenants. This done, he telephoned the police. In fifteen minutes the Divisional Inspector for Kensington arrived, together with a sergeant and two constables. Not long after them came a Divisional Surgeon and then the photograph and fingerprint boys. Whilst they went to work, Divisional Inspector Davidson spent his time strolling about the flat, looking at everything and touching nothing, sketching outlines in his notebook and pooling his results with the sergeant. Then the G.P. came into the main living room where the two men were waiting.

'Well, doc, what happened to her?' Davidson enquired.

'Suffocated — with one of the pillows too, judging from the saliva marks upon it. We can check that at forensic. She's been dead about ten to eleven hours.'

'Any observations on that tattoo mark on her back?' the Divisional Inspector asked.

'That's your province, Davidson,' the doctor shrugged. 'However, I did have a look at it. It isn't recent. I'd say it's been on her back since she was a child.'

'That's guesswork, isn't it?' said the sergeant, whose one passion was facts.

The G.P. gave him an acid look. 'My job doesn't rely on guesswork. I'm stating a truth. When you look at that tattoo closely you can see that the skin pores are distended. To cut it short, the woman grew a good deal after the tattoo was made.'

There was silence for a moment or two after that, then the G.P. snapped the catches in place on his bag. He headed for the door.

'I'll send the ambulance over for the body,' he said over his shoulder. 'After that it can stay at the mortuary pending a p.m. and identification. I'll send in my report to your office.'

He disappeared, and the door closed behind him. Davidson turned and entered the bedroom. The two photographers had come to the end of their work and were packing up their traps. The fingerprint man was busy with one of the pillows, brushing it carefully. Near him stood an insufflator.

'Any luck, Hargreaves?' Davidson asked, glancing at him.

'Nothing that's going to do us much good, I'm afraid.' He shook his head and tossed the pillow back on the bed. 'Fingerprints don't come out properly on that material, so I'm thinking we'll have to rule it out.'

'You mean there are no prints any-where?'

'Plenty — but most of them match up with the dead woman. Those that don't are so smudged as to be useless — a set on the window frame, for instance. Whoever it was wiped them away afterwards, either with a handkerchief or a coat-sleeve. Enough to block us, anyway.'

Davidson sighed. 'Okay, if that's the way it is. Send in what photos you've got to my office. How about you chaps?' he asked the photographers.

'Four positions,' said the man with the camera. 'We'll rush them in to you, Inspector.'

Davidson waited a moment or two until he and the sergeant were left alone. Then he walked slowly to the bed and considered the corpse, and particularly the tattoo in the back. Near him, the sergeant stood with tight lips, thinking.

'Any ideas?' Davidson asked him presently.

'None that make much sense. That tattooed name has me baffled. Why the devil should a woman want to remember another woman? Seems crazy to me.

What is even crazier is having it put on her back like that. It must have meant she'd never have been able to wear a low-cut gown or a swimsuit, and that must have been a considerable drawback to an attractive piece like her. She's got looks, even in death. Strange she never made any effort to have the name removed . . . ' The sergeant leaned closer and studied the tattoo carefully. Then he straightened up again. 'No sign of it being marked with acids or anything of that nature, in an effort to shift it.'

'Yes, it's strange all right,' Davidson confirmed, and looked about him. 'Nothing much in the way of a clue, either. The attacker obviously entered by the window, and that's all we know. All we can do at the moment is go into some routine enquiry. Tell Withers — he's on duty in the corridor — to get the proprietor up here. At the same time have Benson go back to the car. He doesn't need to stand outside the front door: it's giving the place a bad name.'

The sergeant nodded and left the room. The proprietor was soon under the fire of the Divisional Inspector's questions, interviewed in the living room where he could not see the body. As a result of what he learned Davidson appeared in Madame Luchaire's salon towards ten o'clock and, with the sergeant, soon found himself cloistered with Miss Chantry, the sharpnosed secretary.

'I find this most disturbing, gentlemen,' she commented, after she had waved them to chairs. 'Obviously your business must be very important, so if you would care to wait until Miss Bradmore gets here — Madame Luchaire, you know — I am sure she — '

'Miss Bradmore will not be here this morning, or ever again,' Davidson said quietly; then, satisfied that the hardbaked secretary was not the kind to swoon before startling news he added briefly, 'She was murdered in her flat last night.'

Miss Chantry, who had been fishing behind her for her chair, suddenly fell into it and stared.

'Did — did you say — murdered?' she whispered incredulously.

'I did, madam.' Davidson gave her an outline of the facts insofar as the law permitted him; then he added, 'We got some personal details from the proprietor of her flat — hence our presence here. You were closely connected with her, of course, as her secretary?'

'In the business sense, yes.'

'Can you then bring to mind anybody who might have wished to do her an injury?'

'Well I — I hardly think I can . . . ' Miss Chantry stopped and gave a little start. 'Or perhaps I may be wrong!' she corrected herself. 'Yesterday the head saleswoman here was discharged — a Miss Wilton.'

Davidson raised an eyebrow, implying thereby that he might be interested. The secretary hurried on:

'Miss Wilton did not take her dismissal with good grace. In fact she threatened Miss Bradmore before she left.'

'Am I to assume you were present when that happened?' Davidson asked.

'No, but before leaving she did tell me to put an advert in the paper for a new head saleswoman — and also, later on, our woman house detective told me that she had been instructed by Miss Bradmore to keep an eye open for a possible attack by Miss Wilton.'

'Mmmm . . . ' It was impossible to tell whether Davidson was impressed or not. 'I'd better have a word with the house detective, if I may have her address.'

Realizing that the Divisional Inspector was merely being polite whilst issuing a command, Miss Chantry gave him the address immediately — that of a house in Bloomsbury. The sergeant took it down in his notebook, as indeed he had been taking the whole conversation. Then Davidson asked another question.

'Do you know if Miss Bradmore had anybody connected with her by the name of Mary?'

This time the secretary was stumped and looked it.

'Well, then, can you name anybody else connected with her — intimately, that is? Had she any relatives?'

'None that I know of, Inspector. She had a fiancé, though.'

A vague gleam kindled the Divisional Inspector's eyes. 'Had she, though? Whom?'

'His name's Derek Cantrill — a stocks-and-shares broker. At this time of the day you'll find him at Westmore Chambers, Throgmorton Street.'

'Many thanks,' Davidson said, as the sergeant's hand traveled over his notebook. 'Which, for the time being, completes my enquiry here. Since, however, you were so closely connected with Miss Bradmore as her secretary, Miss Chantry, it would be as well if you saw the body and identified it. Just a routine procedure, you understand.'

Miss Chantry looked scared.

'You — you mean, see her corpse?'

'I realize it will not be pleasant, madam, but in the absence of relatives, it has to be done — soon as possible, otherwise I could ask Mr. Cantrill to do it. I have two men in the car outside. They'll soon run you to the mortuary and back. The sergeant and I can walk the short distance to Throgmorton Street.'

Miss Chantry had no choice. A few minutes later Davidson and the sergeant watched the police car whirl her away as, on foot, they made their way towards nearby Throgmorton Street. They drew a blank, however. Derek Cantrill was out of town for the day — so Davidson left instructions for him to report at his Kensington headquarters upon his return.

'I suppose the Wilton woman comes next, then?' the sergeant asked as they returned to the street.

'Yes, and let's hope we have better luck.' Davidson raised a hand to a passing taxi.

To their satisfaction, upon arrival at a boarding house in Conway Avenue, Bloomsbury, they learned from the hard-faced landlady that Claire Wilton was at home. She occupied a quite comfortable furnished flat on the second floor and, obviously ill at ease, admitted both men into the living room.

'Is there — something wrong?' she asked anxiously, motioning to the settee.

'You are Miss Claire Wilton?' Davidson

27

asked, as she seated herself gracefully opposite them.

'Yes, that's right. But I can't imagine what — '

'I'll be to the point, madam. This morning, Miss Vera Bradmore — your late employer, I understand — was found murdered in her Kensington flat. We are conducting an enquiry, of course, which demands interviews with all the unfortunate lady's associates.'

Claire Wilton opened her mouth to speak and then shut it again. A blank, terrified look came in her sultry dark eyes. The sergeant brought out his notebook and put it on his knee. The elastic accidentally shot back with a loud snap.

'I — I just can't believe it!' Claire exclaimed finally. 'Miss Bradmore — dead? Murdered! Are you sure?'

Davidson gave a wintry smile. 'Perfectly sure, Miss Wilton. However, don't be alarmed. I merely wish to ask a few questions.'

'You mean, I'm under suspicion?'

'Frankly, madam, everybody is under

suspicion. That is natural in a case of murder. However, I'll be more explicit, shall I? I believe you were discharged by Miss Bradmore yesterday and were not particularly — er — pleased about it?'

'I considered my dismissal outrageous!' Claire retorted, her nervousness apparently vanishing.

'Might I ask why?'

'I had worked five years for Miss Bradmore and never made any mistakes — then, because I accidentally ripped a costly garment, she discharged me. I thought it decidedly unjust.'

'Mmmm. And, as I understand it, you did not forget to mention the fact.'

'I — er — ' Claire hesitated and looked away for a moment; then her gaze returned to the Divisional Inspector's steely eyes. 'Well, yes,' she said, 'I was so blazing wild I'm afraid I did say a good deal.'

'Apparently you said enough to cause Miss Bradmore to put the house detective on her guard against you returning and causing trouble.'

'Ridiculous!' Claire said.

'True, nevertheless.' Davidson reflected for a moment, then he asked, 'What exactly did you say to her? Did you threaten her?'

'No. I simply said that she hadn't heard the last of the incident.'

'And what did you mean by that?'

'I thought perhaps I might be able to make a case out against her for wrongful dismissal.'

'I see. You didn't openly threaten her, then?'

'Certainly not!' Claire's full mouth set firmly. 'Please don't read more into things than is really there, Inspector!'

Davidson smiled dryly. 'I am simply recalling, Miss Wilton, that your employer considered your parting words ominous enough to instruct the house detective to guard her.'

'That could only be the outcome of her imagination. I had no intention of doing anything violent — nor did I. If you think I had anything to do with her murder, you're vastly mistaken.'

'I didn't say that you had, Miss Wilton. Tell me, what kind of a woman was Miss

Bradmore? You worked side by side with her for five years. Was she pleasant, nasty, capable — or what?'

'Capable enough and a good business woman — but she had a vile temper and, deep down, she was cheap. I found out, purely for the fun of it, where she originally hailed from. Apparently she was born somewhere in the East End.'

'Had she any relatives that you know of?'

'She never mentioned any, and I never discovered anything concerning any.'

Davidson hitched himself slightly forward on the settee.

'Do you know if she knew anybody by the name of Mary?'

'Not that I'm aware of . . . '

Davidson got to his feet. 'Well then, I think that's all, Miss Wilton. Thank you for being so co-operative. All I need now is a résumé of your activities yesterday evening between eight o'clock and midnight.'

Claire rose slowly, that hesitant look coming back into her dark eyes.

'You mean — for the purposes of an

alibi, I suppose?'

'You might call it that,' Davidson admitted gravely.

Claire shrugged. 'I just haven't one. When I left the salon, I came straight home here and didn't turn out again all evening. Nobody saw me arrive — they very rarely do — and I had no callers. So I'm afraid it's a case of your just having to accept my word for it.'

Davidson did not appear in the least perturbed. 'Very well, Miss Wilton, thank you. You were at home here but have nobody who can substantiate the fact. For the moment that will be all, I think — and I'm much obliged to you.'

He delayed no longer. With the sergeant beside him, he re-entered the waiting taxi and returned to his headquarters in Kensington. Here, after he and the sergeant had had their lunch brought in, they considered the data that so far had been gathered. On the desk were the reports from the Divisional Surgeon and fingerprint department, plus a stack of photo-graphs, together with a statement that

Miss Chantry had positively identified the body as that of Vera Bradmore.

'Next comes the inquest,' Davidson said, lighting his pipe, 'which we'll have adjourned pending our investigation. Our job right now is to try and hammer some sense into what we have already.'

He spent some time studying the photographs from the fingerprint department, but none of them was satisfactory in detail. From these he turned to the prints made by the photographers from various parts of the fatal bedroom, which photographs included several shots of the body.

'According to this,' the sergeant said, pushing over the Divisional Surgeon's report, 'there's no doubt that Vera Bradmore did die through being smothered. Saliva test proves it was hers on the pillow and nobody else's. What does that suggest to you, sir?'

'A woman,' Davidson answered, shrugging.

'A woman killer, you mean? Why?'

'Smothering is a favorite method of the female. If you're in doubt about it take a look at Hans Gross's observations some time. A woman rarely has the strength for manual strangulation so, barring the knife or gun attack, smothering is a nice method. It stifles cries and kills the victim. Vera Bradmore was not a woman of great physical power and, in the hands of a stronger woman, might very easily have gone under.'

The sergeant reflected, his eyes on the smoky ceiling.

'You're thinking of Claire Wilton, I suppose?

'She's suspect, of course — a good motive and a rocky alibi. But she's the elegant type and, I imagine, not the athletic sort who might indulge in smothering and climbing up to a fourth floor apartment. As for Miss Chantry, the secretary, she had no apparent motive — and she's the withered apple type who relies more on her tongue for viciousness than her physique. I'm pretty well satisfied that she at least hasn't anything to do with it. If I think otherwise later, I can question her movements.' Davidson sucked at his pipe for a moment or two, then added:

'All we know at present is that somebody — presumably female — entered the dead woman's flat by the window and smothered her. The reason for it is obscure. The only clue — if clue it is — is the name 'Mary' on the dead woman's back. Whether the killer wanted to see that name, or it became revealed through the accidental tearing of Vera's pyjama jacket in the struggle, we don't know.'

'Suppose,' the sergeant hazarded, 'that it actually was Mary who committed the murder?'

'No harm in supposing it, but why should she want to?'

Realizing he'd taken a flying leap up a gum tree, the sergeant went no further. He sat scowling at the photographs, and Davidson smoked in silence for a considerable time. Then he said:

'Working on these lines, sergeant, I don't see us getting anywhere. If we're to leave Claire Wilton out of the reckoning, we have to start looking for the unknown factor — a woman probably — who has not been mentioned so far, somebody in Vera Bradmore's life of whom she never spoke. Until we get the right angle on this 'Mary' tattoo we're in the dark. More I think of it, the more convinced I get that the killer was looking for that name. Look at this photo here — it appears only too obvious that the pyjama jacket was ripped down by the killer, presumably to see that name.'

'Uh-huh,' the sergeant admitted; 'but that wouldn't have necessitated smothering Vera, would it?'

'Depends how much she knew. Probably she had to be silenced.'

Again the silence; then Davidson jerked his chair forward with the obvious intention of getting down to business.

'I'll figure things out as closely as I can on paper,' he said, 'and see what we get. We still have this Derek Cantrill chap to check up on. If there's nothing satisfactory from his story, we'll have to enquire more closely into Vera Bradmore's life . . . '

And with that Davidson set to work whilst, in a corner, the sergeant went to work on his typewriter to transcribe the shorthand notes he had made of the various statements. Later they would have to be signed by the parties concerned.

Altogether, Davidson took until tea-time to work out his various theories, and to judge by the expression on his dogged face, he was not particularly pleased when he had finished, either. There was a baffled look in his eyes — and it remained while he and the sergeant had tea.

The sergeant was upon the point of asking questions when he was interrupted by the arrival of Derek Cantrill. The tea tray was quickly removed to the top of the filing cabinet, and Davidson rose with extended hand to greet the young stockbroker.

'Thanks for coming along, Mr. Cantrill — have a seat.'

Derek Cantrill obeyed, putting his neat bowler on the end of the desk. His pallid, artistic-looking face was unusually somber.

'I think you can dispense with the politeness, inspector,' he said. 'If I hadn't have come here — as ordered — you'd have come after me, wouldn't you? Concerning Vera's murder?'

'So you know about it, do you?'

'It's in the evening papers — just an outline of the facts. I never got such a shock in my life as when I read them on my return to the city this evening. So, when I was informed I must report here, I wasn't at all surprised.'

Davidson considered him. 'Mmmm — well, that simplifies matters, doesn't it? All I want of you, Mr. Cantrill, is a statement concerning Miss Bradmore. You were her fiancé, I understand?'

'Up to last evening, yes. We — er — had a difference of opinion, I'm afraid, and we parted in a rather stormy atmosphere.'

'I see — but not sufficiently stormy for her to renounce her engagement to you. I notice . . . ' Davidson looked at the photographs spread on the blotter. 'I notice she was still wearing her engagement ring when found murdered.'

Derek Cantrill did not waste any time giving every detail of what had transpired in the restaurant. Davidson listened in silence, and then sat musing. 'I thought it better to break things off, Inspector, than

38

maintain an engagement which, had it led to marriage, could only have been unhappy for both of us.'

'But Miss Bradmore saw it differently, eh? She was determined to make you stick to your bargain or else start a lawsuit?'

'So she said.'

Davidson said, 'Are you being entirely frank with me, Mr. Cantrill? What caused this sudden change of heart on your part? Was it really because you had decided you and Miss Bradmore were temperamentally unsuited to each other — or was it because you had met another woman more to your — er — taste?'

'Well, I — ' Derek Cantrill gave a little shrug. 'As a matter of fact, yes. Recently I met Mary Hilliard — a really charming girl and quite well known in society. She had education and artistic tastes. Vera, I regret to say, had none.'

'Mary Hilliard?' Davidson repeated, exchanging a look with the sergeant.

Derek Cantrill nodded and then gave an odd little smile.

'I think I know what is in your mind,

Inspector. You're connecting Mary's name with that tattoo on Vera's back.'

'Frankly, yes,' Davidson admitted. 'And where did you learn about the tattoo?'

For answer Derek Cantrill put an early edition of the evening paper on the desk, motioning to a small column on the front page.

'All there,' he said briefly, and Davidson gave a grim nod.

'Uh-huh, so I see. Those blasted reporters get news in the most extraordinary way. Anyway, it doesn't signify. Tell me, Mr. Cantrill, can you help us in any way regarding this 'Mary' business? Did Miss Bradmore ever give out any hints concerning that tattoo, or a person named 'Mary'?'

'No, never. The whole thing came as a complete surprise to me when I read of it.'

There was a pause. Davidson dug idly in the bowl of his pipe with a penknife blade. Without raising his eyes he said:

'Not to put too fine a point on it, Mr. Cantrill, you had no reason to like Miss Bradmore? Either you would have to marry her and give up all thought of — er

— Miss Hilliard; or else be put in court for breach of promise. A nasty business either way for a man in your respectable position.'

Derek Cantrill gave a slow, puzzling smile. 'You have it summed up perfectly, Inspector. From all of which you are thinking I had good reason for wanting Vera eliminated. You're right — but I didn't eliminate her.'

'I never said you did,' Davidson said, snapping his penknife shut. 'But for the sake of our records, what did you do after Miss Bradmore left you in the restaurant, until about midnight?'

'I walked around thinking things out, returning home about eleven.'

'I see. Did you meet anybody or turn in anywhere?'

Derek Cantrill knitted his brows. 'No. Which makes it bad, doesn't it? No proof that my statement is correct?'

'Such things often happen,' Davidson said. 'It's surprising how few people can prove their movements in an emergency. Don't let it bother you, Mr. Cantrill — er, this restaurant you mentioned.

Which one was it?'

'Vantry's, off the Strand.'

'Thank you. Well, Mr. Cantrill, I think that's all for now. Your statement will be shown to you later, when you will sign it — unless there are amendments to be made. In the meantime, thank you for calling.'

Realizing he was being dismissed, Derek Cantrill got up, shook hands, and went out, easing his bowler onto his fair head. Davidson sat musing, filling his pipe from an oilskin pouch.

'Number two with a rocky alibi and a strong motive, sir,' the sergeant commented. 'Though he hardly fills the bill if we're looking for a woman.'

'Oh, I don't know . . . he's effeminate, dandified. He might even commit a crime in a womanly fashion. It's happened before. However, that's leaping my streams before I come to them. Hop round to Vantry's Restaurant, sergeant, and see what you can dig up. So far we've only Cantrill's word for everything. I'd like something more substantial.'

The sergeant nodded, took down the

tea-tray from the filing cabinet, and left the office. He was away perhaps an hour, during which time Davidson went on making his notes.

Then he looked up expectantly as the sergeant returned.

'Quite a bit of luck, sir,' he announced in satisfaction. 'I managed to have a talk with the waiter who served Cantrill and Vera Bradmore last night. It seems he accidentally overheard most of the row those two had last night — or rather, he couldn't help but do so because the Bradmore woman made no effort to keep her voice down, the restaurant being pretty deserted. No doubt but what she gave Cantrill a run for his money and threatened him with breach of promise.'

'Mmmm . . . good,' Davidson commented. 'Ample motive, anyway. Our next move, sergeant, first thing tomorrow, is to see what we can read into the dead woman's past life. I shan't feel on safe ground until I know what that 'Mary' business means. As for now, I think we're as entitled as anybody else — at this stage — to go home to our own firesides.'

3

About the time the Divisional-Inspector was deciding to wrap things up for the day, Mrs. Elsie Jackson, of 47 Kendal Rise, Surbiton, was reading the evening paper, and it being a fairly late edition there was added information on the front page concerning the 'Kensington Murder.' There was also something that had not been in the earlier issues — a small photograph of the dead woman. The police had not authorized its printing, but neither had they put a veto on it — so there it was . . . It was rather as if Mrs. Elsie Jackson were holding a mirror instead of a newspaper, since her features were identical to those of the murdered woman.

'Extraordinary likeness, my dear . . . '

Elsie became aware of her husband's voice from a great distance — even though in actual fact he was seated across from her in the well-furnished lounge.

The angle at which she held the newspaper was sufficient for him to see what had claimed her attention.

'It gave me quite a shock when I first noticed it,' her husband added, getting up and strolling over to her. 'Of course, it is said that everybody has a double — but I would much prefer that your double were not that of a murdered woman!'

Elsie gave a taut little smile and tossed the paper from her as though the whole business were distasteful. She looked up to find her husband considering her thoughtfully.

'Strange business altogether,' he said, musing. 'The woman actually had a tattoo on her back — name of 'Mary.' What do you make of that?'

'Good heavens, George, what am I supposed to make of it? I'm sure there are far more interesting things to talk about than murder. Besides — ' Elsie glanced at the clock — 'you're going to be late for your club.'

George nodded and half turned, then he frowned. 'You actually don't mind my going?' he asked in astonishment. 'You usually grumble pretty freely about it.'

'Just the privilege of a wife, dear,' Elsie said with a smile. 'You go. I have plenty to do — and letters to write.'

George still looked surprised, but went nevertheless. Elsie remained in her chair, her eyes fixed bleakly on the newspaper lying on the settee nearby, until she heard the bang of the front door as her husband departed. Then, satisfied that she was alone in the house — it being the maid's evening off — she crossed to the telephone and raised it, dialing swiftly.

While she listened to the ringing tone her blue eyes shifted again to the distant newspaper. There settled on her good-looking face an expression of deepening alarm, then suddenly she was all attention as a voice responded in the receiver.

'Janice?' she asked quickly. 'You alone?'

A voice practically identical with her own responded. 'Yes, I'm alone, Elsie. I managed to get Dick to go over to see his uncle. He's been talking about doing it for long enough. I guessed you'd be ringing up.'

'I had to! This is an emergency, which

makes it essential we break our pact to go our separate ways and never communicate. You've read the paper, obviously. You realize what's happened?'

'I think I do, and I find it pretty frightening. Whoever murdered Vera knew about that tattoo on her back. That seems pretty evident.'

'Seems like it,' Elsie admitted. 'I can't think who it could have been, though. It puts us in a terrible spot because, if the killer works things out, we'll come next.'

'Yes,' Janice whispered. 'I'd thought of that. There's one thing I'm thankful for, and that is that Dick doesn't read newspapers in any great detail. He'd noticed the headlines in the paper, of course, and the photo — said she looked a deal like me. As well she might since we are — or were — triplets! However, he knows I have a tattoo on the small of my back which says 'Lil,' so I've been at desperate pains to stop him reading the details of the murder. He'd start thinking things otherwise. I think I've handled him all right so far. Have to trust to luck for the rest. How about you?'

'Safe so far,' Elsie replied. 'I packed George off to his club so I could talk to you. I'm a bit safer than you because he's no idea I have a tattoo on my back; I've taken care never to let him see it. He's a pretty jealous chap, remember, and my tattooed 'Ian' might send him off the deep end wondering who it referred to.'

There was silence between the sisters for a moment, then Janice asked rather plaintively:

'Well, what do we do? You were always the one to direct things amongst the three of us. Do you suppose the best thing would be to go to the police?'

'Great heavens, no! That's the very last thing we must do. You and I have both reached pretty high places in the social climb, and if the police were to get the facts, it would soon spread into the newspapers — then think of the scandal.'

'Yes, but there's another aspect to be considered,' Janice pointed out. 'If we told the police everything, we might safeguard ourselves against possible attack by this killer — for I'm pretty sure things won't stop with that attack on Vera. I'm scared, Elsie — honestly I am!'

'Maybe you are, but we've got to risk it. With our married names it's just possible the killer may pass us by. All I can suggest is that, for the moment anyway, we wait and see what happens.'

'All right,' Janice said. 'But I don't like it. Keep in touch with me, Elsie. Promise me that!'

'I promise,' Elsie said. 'Now I've got to say goodbye and think out what comes next.'

She rang off and returned to the armchair where she settled down to think. She spent the remainder of the evening doing so, and by the time George had arrived home she had made up her mind. She rose from the chair as he came into the lounge.

'Have a good time?' she enquired, smiling.

He looked at her in the light of the big reading lamp.

'Yes — within limits. Look here, Elsie, I just don't understand you! Not only did you fail to raise any objections when I went to the club, but now you even enquire if I enjoyed myself! What's the idea? Are you beating up for something?'

'Probably I am . . . ' Elsie went over to him and twined her long fingers in and out of his tie. She looked up at him archly. 'This may sound strange with the summer not really here yet — but would it matter if we spent a few weeks at the beach house?'

'Huh?' George stared blankly. 'But what on earth for? Who the devil wants to be stuck in a beach house on one of the loneliest parts of the south coast at this time of year?'

'I do. I'm sick of town. Anyway, it isn't so lonely. Worthing's only three miles away in the car.'

'But I've my business to attend to! I can't spend three weeks away there out of the world; I'll lose a pile of money.'

'Nothing to stop you carrying on as usual, is there? You can take me there and leave me.'

'In that desert island?' George shook his head firmly. 'No, m'dear, I won't hear of it. Forget the whole thing. We'll go over when the summer really comes, of course, but — '

'It's late May,' Elsie interrupted, a hardness coming into her voice. 'The weather's quite warm, and I want a change! If you won't come with me, I'll go alone.'

George sighed and finally spread his hands.

'Oh, all right, if that's the way you want it — but I think you're crazy. We'll stay for a week — no longer. And it'll probably be about the longest week I ever spent!'

★　★　★

Towards eleven o'clock the following morning, Divisional Inspector Davidson came to a decision. Leaving the sergeant the duty of taking the various statements to the people concerned and obtaining their signatures, he had himself driven over to New Scotland Yard. Towards noon he was shown into a dingy office overlooking the Thames Embankment.

The man busy at the big desk by the window had a perfectly round head and a haircut suggestive of Wormwood Scrubs. In fact, his crowning glory was more like plush than anything else. Beneath it was a round, cherubic face with high complexion, a disarmingly bland mouth, and a snub nose. Chief Inspector Hancock was anything but handsome, yet there was nothing about him an average person could dislike. In the past, one or two criminals had assumed he was a fool, deliberately misled by his easy-going geniality, and were at this very moment doing fifteen years in the cooler for underestimating the enemy.

'Morning, sir,' Davidson said, prosaic as ever, as he sat down at the desk. 'Glad you can spare me the time for a word or two.'

'Or do you mean relieved?' Hancock suggested, an impish gleam in his light gray eyes. 'When you Divisional chaps come to the Yard, it isn't to make a social call. It's because you're up to your blasted neck in trouble.'

'Matter of fact I am,' Davidson admitted, sighing. 'I've not often found it necessary to call in the Yard to a murder case, but I'm out of my depth this time.'

Chief Inspector Hancock gave a broad grin as he glanced across at the opposite corner, where Sergeant Harry Grimshaw was working at his own desk.

'Hear that, Harry?' he asked with a wave of his hand. 'History is being made! A Divisional man admits he's out of his depth . . . make a note of it and we'll frame it.'

'To me,' Davidson said heavily, who always found the C.I.'s banter decidedly unprofessional, 'this business is serious. Murder always is.'

'Don't you believe it,' Hancock chuckled, fishing out a battered briar pipe from his untidy jacket and sniffing at it delicately. 'Nothing in this world is any more serious than you choose to make it — not even murder. The victim is dead and the killer is scared to death. With those two opposite factors what have we got to be serious about? Anyway, let's have it. It's the Vera Bradmore business, of course.'

Davidson stared in surprise as the Chief Inspector lighted his pipe.

'Matter of fact it is, but how did you — '

'Oh, come, come, man; I'm no Sherlock Holmes. It's the only murder case at present and it's in Kensington — your Division. If you say, 'You amaze me, Holmes!' I'll damned well crown you with the phone directory!'

Davidson cleared his throat as though preparing to sing an aria. Instead he started relating his experiences to date — all in a flat, uninteresting monotone — verifying his statements at intervals by reference to his notebook. Hancock remained silent, except for his noisy pipe. Then Davidson finally branched off into a narration of his latest experience.

'Having got the information that Vera Bradmore hailed from the East End district, I thought I'd better see what her history was — so I checked on the birth records this morning. I found her listed as the daughter of Arthur Bradmore, a fairground employee, and Miriam Hilda Bradmore, also a fairground employee. She was born in Hampstead, in the confines of Barraclough's Fair, twenty-eight years ago.'

'And was murdered the night before last,' Hancock finished, squinting through the window at the cloudy May morning. 'How far does that get you?'

'Doesn't get me anywhere. That's the point. I've plenty of leads and motives, but nothing that seems strong enough to stand up. Since, at the time of her birth anyway, Vera Bradmore had no address other than the Fair, she was evidently as nomadic as her parents. The story about her East End upbringing must have begun in her childhood. I'm having that looked into, but the East End is a big place, and I don't expect much result.'

'If you've got a man prowling around in the vague hope of finding all about one Vera Bradmore in the East End of London, you've definitely had it,' Hancock agreed, still peering outside. 'And if you ask me, it's going to rain.'

Davidson shifted irritably. 'What's that to do with it, sir?'

'Huh? Oh — nothing, as far as Vera is concerned. I was thinking of those new rose bushes I've planted. I noticed this morning they were getting pretty dry.'

Not being accustomed to Hancock's winsome little ways, the Divisional Inspector could only stare blankly until he caught sight of the grinning face of Sergeant Grimshaw. Then he pulled himself together and tried to look stern and solid as usual.

'What,' Hancock asked, switching back with bewildering speed to the matter on hand, 'did you hope to gain by exploring Vera's earlier life?'

'An explanation of the tattoo 'Mary.' I have the feeling that if we can only pin down the woman to whom that name refers we may have something.'

Hancock turned a complete circle in his swivel chair and slowed down as he faced his desk again. 'And what makes you think it may refer to a woman?'

'Perfectly obvious, sir, isn't it? Mary! What more do we want?'

'Are you married?' Hancock asked genially.

'Yes, sir.' Davidson frowned. 'Does it matter?'

'It matters in so far that it's about time you learned a bit of feminine psychology. No woman would ever allow her back to be disfigured with a tattoo — and even less would she allow that tattoo to take the form of another woman's name. It wasn't that Vera Bradmore wanted to perpetuate the name of some child of hers, either, because she was a spinster for one thing, and for another, this doctor's report you have here states that the tattoo was made in childhood. So . . . '

Davidson waited. He would have said, 'So — what?' only he checked himself, realizing it might be misinterpreted as insolence.

'According to this medical report,' Hancock continued, when he had dived at it amidst the litter on his desk, 'the tattoo was put on Vera's back in her childhood. And no attempt has ever been made to remove it, apparently. In other words, she probably had no say in the matter, so I think you can dispense with the notion of looking for somebody named Mary.'

'It's still the name of a woman, sir!'

Davidson protested.

'It's also the name of a ship, a bitch, a species of flower, a train, and in the little sense, a stomach . . . ' Hancock grinned and blinked and patted his rotund middle.

The Divisional Inspector sat back in his chair. He looked as though he wondered if he were dealing with a lunatic.

'So,' Hancock said, shrugging, 'what we have to look for is not this hypothetical Mary, and not into Vera Bradmore's past — but into the motives of those who might be responsible. First, the head saleswoman who was so embittered at her dismissal; second, the almost too glib statements of Derek Cantrill; third, the apparently innocuous secretary, Miss Chantry. All you've done, Davidson, is scratch the surface. You haven't hammered those three folks half enough.'

'Probably I haven't your unique method,' Davidson said acidly.

'There's no doubt of it, you haven't . . . ' Hancock got to his feet and passed a hand over his bristly scalp. 'Tell you what you do, Davidson

— leave this with me. That's what you really want, even if you're not saying so in so many words. But in taking it over, I insist on being left alone. I can't stand being helped — so-called — while I'm on the job.'

'If you're taking it on, sir, it's all yours,' the Divisional Inspector said. 'I know when I'm licked.'

'Okay, then. Have all reports redirected to me, and I'll take on from this point. Tomorrow, probably, there'll be an inquest — which you'll have to attend. I'll be there too and get the thing adjourned pending further investigation — ' Hancock broke off, and his cherubic face gave way to a beaming smile as he looked at the window. 'By gosh, it is raining!' he declared. 'Now I'm really happy!'

'I'll be going then, sir,' Davidson said gruffly and headed for the door. He had been gone some moments before Hancock turned from watching the raindrops on the window to reconsider the reports and photographs on the desk. Going over to them he studied everything in silence, drawing at his evil-smelling pipe.

''Mary, Mary, quite contrary',' he said, his light gray eyes narrowed. 'Between ourselves, Harry, I think we've bitten off something pretty hefty here.'

'Yes, sir,' the sergeant said. 'Yet it seems strange that just a straightforward business of smothering should be so baffling. There have been dozens of such happenings, and the murderer found every time.'

'Yes — but none of them had such an extraordinary motive as this killer seems to have had. It's plain as the nose on my face that that killer wanted to discover that name 'Mary' — and where it fits in, I'll be damned if I know . . . I see that Davidson has made a note here that he suspects a woman because Vera Bradmore was smothered. Doesn't seem to occur to him that a man might have done it, using a woman's technique, to throw us off the scent. Nothing for it, I'm afraid, but to question these people again and try and charm something out of them. I imagine our good friend Davidson would more scare them than anything.'

Hancock went over to the stand and

took down a worn raglan coat and soft hat. He scrambled untidily into the coat and jammed the hat on the back of his bullet head.

'See you later,' he said briefly. 'I'll grab some lunch and then do some interviewing. You might polish off the details of the Brayford case while I'm gone . . . '

★   ★   ★

Towards seven o'clock this same evening Chief Inspector Hancock wandered absently into the Under-Sixty Club adjacent to Whitehall. He was a member of it for no other reason than that he was forty-seven and liked its sepulchral solitude when he needed absolute quiet in which to work out a problem. By this time most of the soft-footed staff knew his square, untidy figure and had come to accept his muteness as part of his stock-in-trade. In here his lighter side was rarely seen, for he never came near unless a problem weighed heavy upon him.

Singling out a red hide chair in the pin-quiet main room, he flung himself into it and sat scowling. His restless hand pushing up over his forehead knocked his hat off and behind his back. He ignored it and then looked up at a hovering waiter as though he wondered whom the man was.

'Evening, Inspector. Anything I can get you?'

'Yes, a brandy-and-soda. God knows I need something to make my brain work.'

The waiter departed and presently returned. Hancock took the drink and tossed it off, then he resumed his scowling, peering through narrowed eyes at the carpet. Not that he saw it. He was plowing again through the interviews he had had during the afternoon. He had got no further than Davidson — except in one respect. It appeared that Derek Cantrill was, on this second occasion, not quite so sure that he could not provide an alibi for his movements. He had asked for a chance to do so — a chance that at this stage Hancock could do nothing but permit.

'Begins to look as though Davidson wasn't so far out after all,' he mused.

'Plenty of leads and all of them going nowhere. That makes the killer an unknown quantity — and if there's one thing that gets me down in these crime puzzles, it's an unknown quantity! No sign of the dead woman ever having been seen with any other woman. No friends apparently. No letters that might help. Why the devil didn't I take my mother's advice and become a nurseryman?'

'Well, well, it's Billy Hancock!'

The Chief Inspector gave a start and looked up. The voice had sounded quite loud — but only because it had interrupted his soliloquy. Nobody dared speak above a hoarse whisper in these hallowed precincts.

The owner of the voice was tall, broad-shouldered, and deeply bronzed. His lounge suit seemed out of place; he would have looked better in a sea captain's uniform.

'Tom Cavendish!' Hancock exclaimed, grinning as he rose to shake hands. 'Well fancy bumping into you after all this time. Damn it, man, I'd given you up for lost. Here, have a seat and a drink. In the meantime, have a cigarette.'

They both sat down again, Hancock offering his cigarette case. When drinks had been brought, the first effusion of the meeting had evaporated. Tom Cavendish, looking incredibly healthy, had the appearance of a man in the late thirties, with his dark waving hair and keen blue eyes. Actually he was no more than thirty-two, with responsibility and many travels directly responsible for the apparent added years.

'Must be two years since I saw you last,' Hancock said, reflecting. 'Up to then I could never get out of your way — especially in here. Eh?'

'Just the way of things.' Cavendish smiled. 'Struck up quite a friendship, didn't we? Things have changed a lot for me, though, since our days of going to the football matches together — and for the better, I'm glad to say.'

'Good. Wish I could say the same. Where have you been putting yourself these last two years?'

'I got myself a good job in the exporting business, and that's made it necessary for me to travel abroad a good deal. I only got back to England two days ago, as a matter of fact. Coming past here today, I thought I'd take a look how things were going on. I had half an idea you might be here. If not, I'd intended to call on you in Whitehall.'

Hancock grinned as he finished his drink. 'I'm in the same old hen-run with the smoky ceiling. If I didn't have my gardening to do and a good wife and kids back of me, I think I'd go stark nuts sometimes.'

'That reminds me . . . I'm no longer a bachelor, Billy. I brought a wife back with me from abroad. Betty by name. Sweet a girl as you ever saw.'

'Gets better as it goes on,' Hancock commented. 'Steadying influence, my lad. Do you good!'

'So she tells me — but I'm afraid I have to leave her alone a good deal, and I don't like it. Not that she bothers. I managed to find a house just our size outside Wimbledon, and she's enjoying fitting it up. The fact that I bought it and have plenty of cash to spare is a measure of my prosperity.'

'I was just thinking I'm in the wrong business,' the Chief Inspector sighed. 'Now I'm sure of it.'

'Anything particular stirring in the morbid world of crime?' Cavendish asked, sitting back in his chair.

'If something would stir I'd be happy — but it doesn't. I'm banging my napper good and hard on a brick wall trying to knock some sense into the Vera Bradmore business.'

'Oh, yes,' Cavendish said, thinking. 'I seem to have read something about it. Smothered, wasn't she — and had a name tattooed on her back?'

'That's the lady. I took it over this morning from a Divisional Inspector who'd had more than enough of it. Now I wish I hadn't been so cocksure. It's a stinger, Tom, believe me! One of those delightful problems that have you rushing round in circles and unable to pin any one aspect down properly. I came in here to think it out — and now look at me.'

'I'd better be on my way, perhaps — '

'Great Scot, no! I'm only too glad to

have you to talk to. Been so long since we exchanged notes. What more have you got to tell me? You don't want to hear me talking shop and murders, surely?'

'But I do! I'm interested! So's Betty.'

Hancock stared. 'She is? Not many women that are.'

'She isn't bloodthirsty, if that's what you're thinking,' Cavendish laughed. 'She just likes pointing out the headline stuff to me over the breakfast table, and when it's crime she reads all about it to see how the police go to work. When I got in this morning she had all the details of this Kensington business off pat from the early editions.'

'Got *in*?' Hancock repeated vaguely. 'From where?'

'I've been up north the last two days seeing sundry people. Only got back into London early this morning.'

'Oh . . . ' Hancock seemed to be thinking of something for a moment. Whatever it was did not take on words, however. He gave his bland smile. 'Wish my missus was as interested in crime,' he sighed. 'She considers I'm in a pretty unpleasant sort of business, and I'm not sure but what she's right.'

After a pause, Cavendish said, 'Any hopes of us getting together again as we used to do? There'll be cricket matches we could see — '

'Later on, maybe,' Hancock said. 'At this moment I've too much tied round my neck to make any arrangements.'

'But I want you to meet the wife, Billy. She's keen on sports, just as I am. In fact she was an athlete herself when in her teens. Look, why don't you come over and spend an evening with us? Nothing she'd like better than meeting a C.I. face to face.'

Hancock grinned. 'Thanks for the flattery. I should think her opinion of inspectors will hit bottom when she sees me. I'm such an uninteresting, untidy old codger. Anyway, thanks for the invitation. The moment I've a free evening, I'm your man. How can I get in touch with you?'

Cavendish got to his feet and handed over his visiting card.

'There it is — with my home telephone number.' He glanced at his watch. 'Now

I've got to be going, Billy. The wife sees little enough of me as it is. I'm always dashing away somewhere. See you again.'

Hancock nodded, got to his feet and shook hands. Before long he too was on his way home, wondering for perhaps the first time since his promotion to Chief Inspector what move he could make next. As far as he could see the inquest was his only hope. During it, the evidence of the various people concerned might give him a fresh angle. Otherwise, there was the horrible possibility that the Kensington Murder might have to be relegated to the 'Case Uncompleted' file.

4

About the time Chief Inspector Hancock was prowling homewards, Claire Wilton was seated in a quiet little café in Bloomsbury. Before her was an anxious-looking young man with sharp features and big hands. On the table there stood tea and sandwiches, neither of which had been touched so far.

'And that's the situation, Terry,' Claire sighed moodily. 'You've seen part of the story from the papers and you can realize what sort of a funk I'm in. That's why I rang you up to come and talk things over with me.'

Terry Baxter, who considered his managership of a garage sufficient backing for wanting to marry Claire, sat thinking for a moment or two. Being accustomed to a practical life in the handling of cars and forthright customers, he had no ability for seeing below the surface of things.

'I honestly don't see what you have the wind-up about,' he said at length. 'Naturally you didn't commit the murder, so why worry? You can't help being suspected, of course — but if your conscience is clear what in the world does it matter?'

'Easy for you to talk,' Claire said sullenly. 'You're not mixed up in this business. Didn't you ever hear of circumstantial evidence? People have been hanged because of it before today.'

'Maybe — but where's the evidence pointing to you having done something?'

'There isn't any; but there is the fact that I haven't an alibi! I went home the night Miss Bradmore was murdered, and I stopped there. Add to that the things I said to her before I left the salon and see how it adds up! I'm scared, Terry — scared to death.'

Terry smiled reassuringly and began pouring out the tea. He pushed over one of the cups slowly.

'Here — have this. Make you feel better. We've got to keep things in focus, Claire, and you know I'll help you in whatever way I can. I still think you're making a mountain out of a molehill.'

'Had it been just one round of questioning I wouldn't have bothered so much,' Claire said slowly. 'But this afternoon I was questioned again — and this time by a Chief Inspector from Scotland Yard. He was a strange sort of chap — seemed to talk more about gardening than anything else, but by the time he'd gone I realized I'd told him everything he wanted to know. There was a strange look in his eyes too when he knew I'd no alibi worth mentioning.'

'Take no notice,' Terry suggested. 'He can think only in terms of facts. Without proof he can't do a thing.'

Claire drank some of her tea, and it was clear from the expression on her face that her anxiety was mounting.

'I — I suppose we couldn't invent an alibi?' she asked. 'You and me between us? If we could prove we were together, or something, on the night of the murder — '

'What!' Terry stared at her in amazement. 'Don't be so crazy! You've already told the police you were at home. If you alter it now you'll make things worse than ever ... anyway, I can't help you there. On the night of that murder I was at the local dramatic society, with about a dozen witnesses to prove it. Nothing we can do there.'

'Then I've only got one course,' Claire said slowly. 'I'm going to pack my traps and get out.'

'And go where?'

'Up north somewhere. Lose myself. I'm convinced the police think I finished Miss Bradmore, and my bad alibi gives them all the chance they need to pin something on me.'

'And you're kidding yourself that they won't find you? Don't be such a fool, Claire!' Terry's fingers gripped her hand tightly. 'You'll only make things infinitely worse by doing that. Anyway, you can't. There'll be an inquest soon and you'll have to attend it.'

'And get myself hammered down even more than I am now? No thanks! I'm not going anywhere near that inquest — '

'But failure to attend it is an offence! You must!'

Claire said nothing. She sat looking morosely at her tea-cup. Then Terry's hand tightened on her fingers again.

'Listen, Claire, I can understand your feelings,' he said gently. 'I'd probably feel the same if things were banked up against me as they are against you — but no good was ever done by running away from responsibilities. You've got to go through with it. Tell the truth and leave it at that. The law's fair enough if you really are innocent.'

'I wish I could believe that,' Claire sighed. 'Justice miscarries sometimes, as it easily could in this instance . . . I'm in such a horrible mess all round. I'm suspected of murder; I can't apply for a fresh situation anywhere with things hanging over my head, and I've plenty of financial responsibilities that relied on my job at the salon to be met. I'm just — down and out. For the moment.'

'As long as I'm around you'll never be that,' Terry assured her. 'Rely on it. But you've got to hang on. Promise me?'

'I'll . . . try.' Claire hesitated, her dark eyes moody. 'Yes, I'll try. I'm not committing myself any further than that.'

'Good enough. Now try and eat some of these sandwiches. Otherwise you're going to starve yourself to death . . . '

⋆ ⋆ ⋆

The following morning each party concerned received notice to attend the inquest that afternoon in the Kensington Coroner's Court at 2 p.m. Such an order did not affect Elsie Jackson, making her last minute plans for departure to the south coast cottage by the eleven o'clock train. In the background George hovered, by no means looking forward to the isolation the cottage would enforce. Back of his mind was a profound bewilderment. He just could not understand why his wife had so suddenly made up her mind to leave town — nor why she had made no plans for her return. It was as though she were running away from something . . .

'Personally, I think it's crazy!' he declared flatly, as he came to the end of a good deal of mental research.

Elsie looked at him from the opposite end of the lounge. She had just finished closing the bureau where she had been sorting correspondence that, presumably, she intended to deal with at the cottage.

'We're not going into all that again, are we?' she asked sharply.

'At least I'm surely entitled to an explanation?' George came forward, his face harassed. 'I know women do strange things and get sudden whims — but this is beyond all reason. Who are you afraid of all of a sudden?'

Elsie gave a little start and hoped it had not been noticed.

'Afraid of? Why, nobody! Why should I be?'

'I'm asking you, Elsie! The way you've decided on this exodus is beyond everything! It conveys the impression to me that you're just packing up your traps and running for it.'

'Well, I'm not,' Elsie told him deliberately. 'I simply want a change, that's all.'

'Well, I'm still in two minds whether to come with you or not. I've some important business pending, and I'll probably lose it if I shut myself away down at the cottage.'

'I'm going anyway,' Elsie said immovably. 'By the eleven o'clock train.' Then realizing her adamancy might seem altogether too abnormal, she added, 'I've — I've got an idea for a book, if you must know. I want peace and quiet and no callers so that I can write it.'

George considered her sourly. 'That's a good one. Takes you all your time to write a decent letter. Disadvantage of a poor upbringing, I suppose.'

It was not often George dug up her lack of refinement so brutally. Obviously he was only doing it now in an effort to hit back for the inconvenience he was being caused.

'You wanted an explanation,' Elsie snapped. 'Now you have it! I can't make you believe it!'

'Which is a wonder. You seem to be able to make me believe most things.'

'Look here, George, I've had about enough of your confounded — ' Elsie broke off and simmered down abruptly, glancing towards the doorway. 'Yes, Ella, what is it?' she asked curtly.

'The taxi for the station, mum,' the maid said. 'It's just arrived'.'

'Very well. We're coming.'

The maid departed and Elsie gave her husband a direct look.

'If you want to back out you've still got the chance,' she said.

George shook his head slowly. 'No, I'll come. If anything important happens Ella will be here to pass it on to me down at the cottage.'

Elsie, in her movement towards the door, paused and looked back.

'But I told her she could go home until we needed her again — with pay, of course.'

George gave a grim smile. 'So she said. I changed it. I'm not letting her idle her time indefinitely on my money. She can stay here and get the mails and readdress them. I don't intend being cut off from all civilization, even if you do.'

Elsie hesitated, but she did not say any more. She turned and went into the hall. With an impatient movement George began to follow her.

* * *

Around noon, Derek Cantrill was waiting outside a restaurant in Kensington where he was a complete stranger. Since the murder of Vera Bradmore, he had deserted his own haunts so that his movements could not be watched — by those who knew him, anyway. He knew perfectly well it was no use trying to hide anything from the police. They probably had tabs on him all the time.

He had been waiting perhaps ten minutes when a black Daimler drew in to the curb. The chauffeur alighted, and from the limousine stepped a slim, fashionably dressed dark young woman. Immediately Derek Cantrill hurried over to her, raising his bowler as he did so.

'Thanks for coming, Mary,' he said gently, taking her slim hand. 'I wouldn't have bothered you except for urgency. We can lunch here,' he added, glancing towards the restaurant.

Mary Hilliard nodded composedly, instructed the chauffeur to go for his own lunch in the interval, then preceded

Derek Cantrill through the glass swing doors. When they were seated at a quiet table she drew off her gloves slowly and contemplated him with some wonder in her dark eyes.

'I had to make a special effort for this, Derek — and put off an appointment as well. Not that I mind ... but I am wondering why.'

The arrival of the waiter held things up for a moment or two while the menu was consulted; then, plainly worried, Derek said quietly:

'I'm in the most horrible spot, Mary — and before you get any news the hard way I thought it best to tell you everything.'

'Oh?' Mary Hilliard was not the kind of girl to show surprise easily. She waited with still the look of mystification on her aristocratic features.

'I suppose you've ... read of the Kensington murder?' Derek asked, hesitating.

'Not very thoroughly. I've seen the headlines, of course, but crime hasn't the slightest interest for me ... ' Then it occurred to Mary what an extraordinary question Derek had asked. Her expression changed. 'What in the world has the Kensington murder got to do with it?' she asked blankly.

'I'm involved in it,' Derek muttered. 'Innocently, of course. So far the papers haven't mentioned the names of suspects, but I'm one of them.'

The girl was silent, gazing fixedly. There was neither resentment nor horror in her eyes. She looked plain stunned.

'Knowing you as I do,' Derek said, 'I think you should have the facts. If you don't, you will in time through the papers. When I met you I was . . . engaged to Vera Bradmore.'

'Was that what you meant by an attachment which you said didn't mean anything?'

'That was it. I was perfectly sure I'd have no difficulty in breaking things off with Vera — only she didn't see it my way.'

Mary raised an eyebrow and the temperature dropped several degrees. The waiter came and brought the meal.

Perfectly composed, Mary picked up her knife and fork.

'Not very straightforward in your statements, Derek, were you?' she asked quietly.

'I expect you to be angry, and I deserve it,' he answered. 'I only hope that my admission of the facts now — openly, without you hearing them through other ways — will prove how much regard I have for you.'

'If things had worked as you'd intended, and you had been able to break things with this unfortunate girl, were you intending that we should become engaged without your earlier engagement ever being mentioned to me?'

'I'd intended telling you everything, Mary. I swear to that.'

The girl said nothing. She went on eating daintily without looking up. Derek compressed his lips.

'This afternoon there is an inquest,' he continued. 'And that is one reason why I asked you to meet me beforehand. I'm in desperate need of an alibi for the night Vera Bradmore was murdered. I've told the police that I went for a walk — which I did — but I can't prove it because I didn't meet or speak to anybody. Now I have added the statement to Scotland Yard that perhaps I can prove my alibi. And I can . . . if you'll help me.'

Mary's expression was not particularly cordial. She looked up briefly but passed no comment. It was plain that the revelations concerning Vera Bradmore had hit her far harder than Derek Cantrill had ever imagined they would.

'If you could say at the inquest that you met me at eleven o'clock outside Regent's Park — which is far enough away from Kensington to be a perfect alibi in every sense — all suspicion would drop from me.'

Mary looked at the thin-featured, artistic face across the table. She saw impatience cross it, as she still remained silent.

'Why on earth don't you say something?' Derek demanded. 'Or don't you grasp what I'm asking you to do?'

'Only too well, Derek. And I'm glad of this chance to see the other side of your nature in time.'

'What in the world do you mean by that?'

'Up to the moment when you told me about Vera Bradmore I had a great respect for you, Derek. I thought you were a decent, good-natured fellow and that we could really make something of life together. In a few seconds you destroyed the whole illusion. Or is it that you think I'm a fool? Can't you see how supremely selfish you are?'

'Selfish? The boot's on the other foot, isn't it? I'm asking you to help me out of a mess, and you're refusing, I suppose?'

'I most certainly am!' Mary did not raise her voice in the least. Her expression was quite enough — cold, indifferent, even contemptuous. 'Apart from the fact that I'd be telling lies in a Coroner's Court, which is a serious offence, I'd be unable to substantiate my statement. On the night of the murder, I was playing bridge with friends until midnight. They would very soon say so, too . . . but even if that fact did not arise, I wouldn't help you, Derek, because you're not the kind of man I thought.'

'Oh, I'm not?' He smiled sourly.

'You were engaged to Vera Bradmore and never told me a thing about it beyond referring casually to an attachment, which I assumed was merely a passing fancy. You tried to break it off with that girl and she, quite rightly, wouldn't let you. You should have stuck to your bargain. If you could do that to her — and it's pretty plain that you're not in the least disturbed by her horrible death — you could do it to me the moment some other girl happened to take your fancy. I'm not taking that risk. Fortunately, we are not yet engaged, and now we never will be.'

An ugly twist came to Derek Cantrill's face. It was surprising how it changed him.

'I'm not the first man to change his mind about a woman!' he snapped.

'Granted, Derek — but as far as I'm concerned you'll never have the opportunity.' Mary rose, quietly serene, and considered him. 'I hardly think I can state it more clearly than that,' she added.

'But, Mary, if you'd only overlook this one lapse — .'

Derek stopped. She took no further notice of him. Without even a handshake, she turned and went gracefully to the swing-doors. He watched her disappear outside and then he sat down again slowly, staring first at her unfinished meal then back to his own untouched one. Only very gradually did he realize that the very thing he had done to Vera had now been done to him.

He gave up all thought of eating, and lighted a cigarette, drawing at it viciously.

★   ★   ★

Ella, the maid to the Jacksons, was entertaining her confectioner boy friend in the kitchen quarters of the residence when the distant shrilling of the telephone interrupted her tête-à-tête.

'Oh, blast!' she complained, rising from the confectioner's knee. 'I thought when the boss and his missus cleared out that I'd get a bit of peace. Some hopes I've got.'

'Better go an' answer it, love,' the confectioner advised. 'Surprisin' how

86

nasty some bosses get when you don't do what you're paid for. I know. Anyway, I'll see you tonight at the Rialto — if you can come?'

'Course I can!' Ella retorted, heading for the kitchen door. 'Don't s'pose I'm stickin' in here all evening by myself, do you . . . ?' She made her way down the broad hall and lifted the phone, switching her voice to quiet respect. 'Hello? The Jackson residence.'

'Oh, could I speak to Mrs. Jackson, please?'

'Sorry madam — or is it sir?' She hesitated, unsure whether a contralto woman or an alto man were speaking. The voice was curiously muffled, which, considering a handkerchief was stretched tautly over the mouthpiece at the other end of the line, was scarcely surprising.

The speaker failed to clear up the mystery of sex and added, 'It's most important. Where can I get hold of her?'

'I'm afraid she's away,' Ella explained, frowning. 'She left this morning and won't be back for an indefinite time. If there's any message I can take — '

'How about Mr. Jackson? Where can I get in touch with him? It's urgent business concerning both of them.'

'He went with her.'

'Where to?'

'I — I'm not supposed to say. They want to be quiet like.'

There was a sound like an annoyed ejaculation at the other end of the wire.

'Confound it all, girl, don't I keep telling you this is urgent? I must see them. Where are they?

Ella saw no point in holding out any longer.

'They've gone to their beach cottage at Lancing — or rather just outside it. Anyway, it's on the shore by itself. The proper address is Seaview Cottage, Lancing.'

'Thank you,' the voice said. 'Thank you very much.'

'Can I have the name, please?' Ella asked. 'I'd better do so that I can — ' She stopped as the receiver clicked at the other end. Pursing her lips she put the phone down on its cradle. When she got back to the kitchen, she found her boy friend had gone so she spent a few minutes reviling the unknown caller who had upset a pleasant half hour.

5

'The more I see of this place, the deader it seems to get! Just look at it! Open sands, empty sea, and not a soul in sight!'

George Jackson, feeling very inappropriately dressed in flannels, considered the view from the one living room of the beach cottage. Some three hours had passed since he and Elsie had arrived, and already he was commencing to feel profoundly bored. Being a man of action, he found it intolerable to have to deliberately kill time. It made things even worse when he thought of the money he might be losing. This, however, was more or less ego. He was the owner of a chain of cut-price stores and the staffs continued to run things whether he lent his presence or not.

'For heavens' sake, George, stop grumbling for a change!' Elsie protested. 'I'm getting sick of listening to you!'

He turned from the window to look at her. She was sprawled in a basket chair, her feet resting on a somewhat worn hassock. George could only see the top of her blonde head. Her face was hidden by the magazine she was reading.

'I thought you came here to write a book,' he said, throwing himself down languidly on the couch. 'You don't seem to be making much of a start.'

'Inspiration doesn't come that easily, George. I have to work myself up to it.'

'How long do you suppose that'll take?'

Elsie lowered her magazine. 'Why on earth don't you go for a walk, or tidy the garden, or something?'

'What? This cabbage patch — ruined by sea water? Like hell!'

'Well, leave me alone, then! If all you can do is grumble, you might as well keep quiet because I'm not going back to the town — and that's final!'

George sighed and put his hands behind his head.

'Only hope for me, then, is that Ella will tell me something important is wanted,' he reflected. 'Or else, she'll send somebody down here which will relieve the monotony.'

Elsie, who had resumed reading, suddenly lowered the magazine again. There was a startled look on her face as she stared at her husband's reclining form.

'Send somebody down here?' she repeated. 'I gave her implicit instructions that she was not to tell a soul where we'd gone!'

'Yes, I know you did — but it struck me as carrying secrecy too far; and there's no earthly need of it just because you want to write a book, if that *is* the reason, which I doubt. You forget that I may have important business decisions to make — so I told Ella that in a case of extreme urgency she could say where we were.'

'You damned fool!' Elsie shouted, leaping to her feet.

George was too astonished to be annoyed. He turned up an eye towards his wife's, angry face. He read fear in it, too, and back came the suspicions into his mind. Frowning, he straightened up and looked at her.

'What on earth is the matter with you, Elsie?' he demanded. 'I've been thinking for some time that there's something strange going on and now I'm becoming sure of it. As for my being a damned fool — well, I'm still a businessman, am I not? I've humored you so far; the least you can do is humor me in case something important turns up.'

Elsie clenched her fists and glared at him. She seemed about to say something, but refrained. Suddenly she turned away and went into the little bedroom, slamming the door. George looked at it, shrugged, and fished his cigarette case out of his pocket.

'I know women take a bit of under-standing,' he said, 'but I seem to have got an extra tough proposition to deal with . . . I never saw such goings-on. Most men would have clipped her on the chin by now.'

He settled back again on the couch, smoking slowly, lost in an abyss of boredom. His cigarette was half burned down when Elsie reappeared, a gaudily colored bathing wrap over her swimming trunks and halter.

'Maybe I'll get a bit of peace if I go for a swim,' she said curtly, pushing the last strand of blonde hair under the rubber cap. 'Certainly there's none in here.'

'You'll find it chilly — and the tide's going out. Don't get caught in it.'

'Would you care very much if I did?'

George swung up from the couch, dropped his cigarette and ground his heel on it. His hands reached out and caught Elsie's shoulders.

'Look, Elsie, do we have to go on this way?' he pleaded. 'I know we pull each other to bits most of the time — but it's mainly in fun. I also know I say things I shouldn't sometimes, like raking up your lack of refinement, and such. But I don't really mean them. We've been more or less happy in our married life, haven't we?'

'I suppose so,' Elsie said indifferently.

'Well, then, what are we squabbling about? All because I told Ella to let people know where we are if necessary. It can't matter that much, can it?'

'Oh . . . leave me alone!' Elsie pulled

herself free and left the cottage by the open main door. The mid-afternoon sun was passably warm. George watched her go, then despondently resumed his reclining attitude on the couch.

Since boredom's ultimate object is to send the victim to sleep, George very soon succumbed. He found himself stirring stiffly at length and opened his eyes to discover that the sunlight had shifted position considerably and had now risen to the opposite wall. It must be early in the evening. Lazily he dragged round his wrist and looked at his watch. It was ten minutes past six.

'Time we had tea,' he muttered, struggling up. 'About the only exciting thing there is to look forward to . . . Hey, Elsie! What about something to eat?'

Realizing she was not in the living room, he looked towards the closed bedroom door as he called. The lack of response got him on his feet, yawning. He shuffled across and opened the bedroom door. Elsie was not in sight.

By degrees he became fully awake and moved more swiftly. Two hours had passed since Elsie had said she was going for a swim.

'Probably sunning herself somewhere,' he muttered. 'Since she has the hump she's liable to do anything to make me alarmed. But hell — two hours! And it's getting nippy, too . . . '

He had reached the sand and shingle outside by the time he had finished talking to himself. He looked about him, but the space was empty. Overhead a lonely gull squawked at him and went into a graceful nose-dive.

'Elsie!' George yelled, cupping his hands. 'Hey — *El-seee!*'

There was no response. The tide was a long way out now, about at the uttermost ebb, the low evening sun glittering in the waves.

Here, alone, George forgot all about the quarrels he had had with Elsie. After all, she was his wife, and in spite of her foibles and his own impetuous nature he loved her. If she had taken things too seriously and walked out on him —

No, that couldn't be it. He recalled, as he walked aimlessly calling her name, that her particular suitcase had been in the bedroom as she had left it. She must be somewhere around here. Perhaps sun-bathing and fallen asleep, as he had . . .

Then he saw her. At first he couldn't believe it. She was perhaps a quarter of a mile away, a lone, brightly colored figure lying in the sand. That was it — lying! George began running at top speed, slowing down from sheer incredulous horror as he came nearer. Finally his run had dragged almost to a standstill. He moved near the silent body.

Elsie was lying face downward, her arms flung wide; her slender ankles crossed over each other. There was no sign of her beach-wrap — just the back of the gaudy halter and trunks. The horrible thing that was her face was buried to the ears in the still wet sand.

'*Elsie!*' George shrieked, plunging suddenly upon her and dragging her head and shoulders up into his arms. 'El — '

He stopped. The face looking at him was dead. No doubt about it. Little blobs of wet sand fell away from it and the blue eyes stared like glass. Dazed, George followed the line of her graceful figure to her back. The broad band of the halter, he saw, had been torn away revealing, a single tattooed word across the spine — 'IAN.'

For a second or two the fascination of looking at it outweighed everything else. He had never seen it before. When he had been swimming with Elsie, she had always had a broad back to her halter, so that it covered the center of the spine completely. George shifted position slightly. The halter, with nothing to secure it, fell away from Elsie's stiffening body.

After that, George did not remember much more. He was in a complete daze. Somewhere at the back of his mind he remembered that a body should not be touched until the police had seen it. No guarantee that this was murder, of course. It could be suicide. But in any case it was a matter for the authorities. So George left the body where it was, reasonably satisfied that in this deserted region nobody would come across it, and the tide would not reach it for another four hours at least.

Then he went to the nearest call box and telephoned the police. They arrived promptly enough and the body was transported to the beach cottage. To the police, however, circulated through the *Police Gazette* with information concerning the murder of Vera Bradmore — and a request to report all details likely to assist the Yard in their investigation — there was a definite parallel between the deaths of Vera Bradmore and Elsie Jackson, a parallel further intensified by the tattoo of 'Ian' on Elsie Jackson's back.

So the information was relayed to Scotland Yard and Chief Inspector Hancock, anxious for the slightest lead to give him a chance to turn round, came to Lancing by the first available train. It was around nine o'clock when he found himself in the oil-lighted beach cottage, Sergeant Harry Grimshaw beside him. On the sofa, still apparently too dazed to think straight, sat George. Beside the table stood an inspector and sergeant from the local constabulary.

'I've got everything made out in a report, sir,' the local man said, as

Hancock put his battered old trilby down on the table. 'Here it is . . . '

He handed over the sheets, which had been typewritten at headquarters. Hancock considered them and nodded.

'And doctor's report?' he questioned.

'That'll be coming shortly. I had him examine the body, of course, and he said asphyxia due to drowning. But there were bruise marks on the back of the woman's neck.'

'There were, eh? And photographs?'

'Yes, those have been taken, too,' the inspector said. 'Before the body was moved. Not do us much good, I'm afraid. There was no sign of a footprint anywhere — except those of Mr. Jackson here, going from this cottage to the body and then coming back again.'

Hancock spent a few more minutes gathering details and then the local men departed so he could handle matters in his own way. He sat down and brooded over the notes that had been given him, then his light gray eyes lifted to where George was watching him morosely.

'Most unhappy business, sir,' he said,

musing. 'And of course it was murder — not suicide. According to your statement here to the local inspector you thought suicide was the explanation.'

'Why should anybody want to murder her?' George asked dully. 'She was a good sort was Elsie. A bit individual at times, perhaps, but nothing more.'

'For that matter,' Hancock said, 'why should she want to suddenly commit suicide? You must have had a reason for thinking she wanted to.'

'We . . . quarreled. It occurred to me that perhaps she had taken things too seriously and put an end to everything.'

George got up and began to pace the small room restlessly. The cold eyes of Hancock followed him. In a corner Sergeant Grimshaw was busy with his pencil and notebook.

'The murder of your wife, Mr. Jackson, is not just a crime on its own,' Hancock said at last, rising, and rubbing a hand over his plush haircut. 'It is, I'm convinced, definitely connected with the murder of one Vera Bradmore in Kensington.'

George came to a stop in his pacing, and wheeled round, his face pale and strained.

'Great heavens, now I remember something! I recall seeing a photograph of a woman in the papers who had been murdered — a woman enough like my wife to be her twin. And . . . ' he finished, staring in front of him, '*she* had a tattoo on her back. A name of some sort. Just the same as my wife has.'

'Exactly so. In Vera Bradmore's case the name was 'Mary.' In your wife's case it is 'Ian'.' Hancock frowned and bit his lower lip pensively. 'Does that suggest anything to you, Mr. Jackson?'

'Not a thing. I don't know anybody named 'Ian,' and I don't think my wife did, either. I didn't even know she had that tattoo on her back until I saw it this evening as she lay on the beach.'

'Did anything happen prior to this tragedy which might have suggested your wife knew her life was in danger?'

'Definitely, yes,' George declared grimly. 'She insisted on leaving town and coming here for an indefinite stay — a crazy idea, as it seemed to me, so early in the summer. When I got too pressing, she said she wanted quiet to write a book.'

'You mean you think she was afraid of something or somebody?'

'I was more than convinced of it . . . ' And without being asked, George went into a full account of everything that had happened. By the time he had finished Hancock was back in the basket chair by the window, sucking gently at his evil-smelling pipe. George finished up on the sofa, his head in his hands.

'Interesting,' the chief inspector commented finally. 'Very interesting . . . Returning to the moment when you found your wife, you are perfectly certain you didn't see anybody?'

'Everything was as deserted as a desert island,' George muttered.

'And there were no footprints,' Hancock muttered, frowning.

He got to his feet and went over to the door. Without explaining himself, he stepped out into the night and didn't come back for perhaps fifteen minutes. As he stepped into the glow cast by the oil lamp, he looked rather less mystified.

'I think the best thing you can do, Mr. Jackson, is stay on here until after the inquest, which will be tomorrow or the day after — '

'With my wife's body in the next room there? The only bedroom, incidentally. No thank you, inspector!'

'The body will be removed,' Hancock said. 'I'll have an ambulance sent over. In any case, it will have to go to the mortuary at Worthing where the Coroner can see it. Now to something else. Was anybody aware that you and your wife had come to this cottage?'

'I told the maid she could reveal where we were to anybody who had really urgent business; otherwise she was to keep it dark. Apparently my wife had insisted that nobody should have our address, but I thought that was absurd. Now I can understand why she did it. She was obviously afraid of somebody.'

'Obviously. And nobody has been here?'

'Not a soul, as far as I'm aware. Unless somebody came when I was asleep and I didn't hear them. I'll never forgive myself for going to sleep like that!' George clenched his fists. 'Had I stayed awake, or even joined my wife in a swim, she would be alive now.'

'Your quarrel,' Hancock said, sniffing at his extinguished pipe, 'was because you had told the maid she could hand on the address of this cottage? That was what you said, wasn't it?'

'Yes. We didn't quarrel often though we — well, had different points of view.'

'Uh-huh. And had your wife any relatives?'

'She never referred to any — beyond saying her father and mother had been dead many years.'

'She never referred to a twin sister, for instance?'

'You're thinking of Vera Bradmore, of course?' George asked, bewildered. 'No, she never mentioned a twin.'

Hancock brooded as he lighted his pipe, then a thought seemed to strike him.

'When you were married, what was your wife's maiden name?'

'She gave it as Elsie Cartwright.'

'I am beginning to think that that name was false, Mr. Jackson. Or else there is a most extraordinary coincidental likeness between Vera Bradmore and your wife. However — that is my problem. I've done all I can here. You'll be good enough to follow out my instructions and stay here until advised otherwise. I'll see to it that the body is removed and that a constable is left on guard in case there might be some further attack directed against you.'

'Why me?' George asked blankly. 'I've no enemies.'

'Not that you are aware of,' Hancock said. 'I prefer not to take chances.'

★   ★   ★

By eleven o'clock, all details concerning the Lancing cottage in the charge of the local police for the time being, Hancock and Sergeant Grimshaw were in the train on their return trip to London. Hancock sat huddled in a corner of the compartment, his pipe crackling aggressively and his trilby pushed back on his bristly scalp.

106

'To me,' Grimshaw said, rubbing his ear after he had been through his notes, 'this looks like one of the toughest things we've bitten off in some time, sir. I can't begin to make head or tail of it.'

'Like the Chinese mystery bulbs in my greenhouse,' Hancock grinned. 'I don't know which is root and which is flower.'

Grimshaw looked across at him and waited. He was glad to find his superior in a droll mood. It usually meant that he was quite satisfied with things to date. His seriousness, in keeping with a dead body in the next room while he had been at the cottage, had now evaporated.

'One hell of a tangle, I admit,' he said, sucking in a mouthful of smoke. 'Yet I'm glad to get a second lead because we can perhaps tie it up with the Vera Bradmore business. Briefly, we're not hamstrung any more.'

'We're not? I thought we were worse off than ever. We've another tattooed body to deal with and an extra suspect added — meaning George Jackson, of course.'

'Why him?' Hancock asked lazily.

'Why not? He quarreled with his wife;

his only alibi is that he was asleep — which isn't an alibi at all — and he had a lonely spot in which to do her in had he wanted. Don't forget the marks on the back of her neck. Those point to the fact that her face was jammed in the wet sand until she suffocated.'

'Exactly. In other words, the same technique of smothering as was used on Vera Bradmore. No, Harry, I don't think George Jackson killed his wife — though I'm open to correction if later evidence points in his direction. I don't think, either, that he would have called the police so quickly had he been the guilty party. In the years I've had of summing people up I never saw anybody so genuinely distressed — and it wasn't acting, either.'

Grimshaw nodded, but he did not look over-convinced.

'What beats me,' he said after a while, as the train swung over the points, 'is why the killer left no footprints. Makes me think we're dealing with a ghost.'

'Then think again, Harry. We're not dealing with anything supernatural, but with a clever, wary, and ruthless killer. As to the puzzle of the missing footprints, that is simply explained. You'll recall I left the cottage for a while and went out into the night?'

'Uh-huh. I rather wondered about that.'

'I went to see what the tide was doing . . . ' Hancock blew through his pipe and watched fine ash ascend to the glowing bulb in the carriage roof. 'It was coming in — which means it was going out all afternoon. There were no footprints from either Mrs. Jackson or the killer. The answer to that one is that she was probably coming out of the sea after her dip when she came face to face with her killer. The killer also walked in the waves when she smothered Mrs. Jackson. Consequently, by staying in the waves until she had got well clear of the spot, the killer destroyed her footprints. The tide would wash the footprints level with the sand and leave no trace. When George found the body the tide had gone back a long way, which made things more mystifying than ever.'

'Yes, sir, sounds reasonable,' Grimshaw agreed. 'And I notice you're still sticking to the feminine gender.'

'No reason to change it,' Hancock grinned. 'I still think a woman is back of this lot because the technique is so female each time. I'm quite aware that a man could make his work look like that of a woman, but somehow that notion doesn't hold together when I come to think about it.'

After some thought, Grimshaw said: 'The woman — assuming you're right, sir — must have left some footprints somewhere. She wouldn't have walked in the sea all the time.'

'True enough — but to try and find them at night is too much like hard work, and I haven't the time anyway. In any case I left instructions with the local police to examine the beach thoroughly beyond the tide line the moment dawn breaks. They may find something; they may not.'

'What's our next move then, sir?'

'To see the maid at Jackson's town home, naturally. It seems pretty certain that she must have handed on the address to somebody, and if we can only get some idea who that somebody was we'll be well on our way to getting somewhere. First thing in the morning we'll go into the matter. Things can't get much worse until then.'

More than this Hancock refused to say. He dragged a seed catalogue out of his overcoat pocket and spent the remainder of the journey studying it intently.

6

It was ten o'clock the following morning when Hancock presented himself at the Jackson residence in Kendal Rise, Surbiton. The maid Ella promptly opened the door and then looked puzzled.

'You'll be Ella, of course?' Hancock asked pleasantly.

'All right, so I'm Ella,' the girl answered curtly. 'What do you two gents want here?'

'Information, my girl.' Hancock showed his warrant-card and then put it back in his pocket. 'Shall we go inside?'

Ella had no choice. Mystified, she led the way into the lounge and motioned to chairs. Then she stood waiting, her expression clearly showing that she wondered what on earth was the matter. She had no means of having a clue to the situation, Hancock realized, because the Worthing police had put a ban on all newspaper information as yet in case it helped the criminal to know what was afoot.

'This will be a shock to you, my girl,' the Chief Inspector said, studying her with his light gray eyes. 'Your mistress was murdered yesterday afternoon at the beach cottage while Mr. Jackson was asleep.'

Ella's eyes opened wide. 'Mur-murdered!' — she repeated at last, aghast. 'But whoever would want to — ?'

'That is what we're trying to find out, Ella, and we're hoping you can help us. The killer could only have known the address of the cottage if you handed it on. That right?'

'Yes, I suppose it is, sir,' Ella agreed animatedly. 'But honestly I never for a moment thought that — '

'Take it easy, Ella,' Hancock said, smiling. 'Sit down and compose yourself. I know servants shouldn't in the presence of visitors — but I'm a servant too. Of the public . . . ' Hancock's grin widened all the more, and Ella nervously edged herself on to a nearby chair.

'Good,' the C.I. commented, sitting

back comfortably. 'Now — don't wrap anything up. Just tell me who it was asked for the address of the cottage. Somebody must have.'

'Yes, sir, indeed they did. I didn't know at first whether it was a man or a woman — but later I found out. It was a woman.'

Hancock said nothing, but he shot a triumphant look at Sergeant Grimshaw as he made his notes.

'First there was a phone call,' Ella explained — and went into detail concerning the incident, suppressing, however, the information that she had been disturbed while necking with her boy friend. 'Then later on the woman herself came and said she'd decided not to go to the cottage after all — that her business could be held over until the master and mistress returned.'

There was silence for a moment. Hancock stirred slightly and contemplated a clump of flowering bulbs in an art pot on the table.

'Late for hyacinths,' he commented. 'Lovely blooms, though.'

The maid stared at him. Grimshaw

stopped writing and waited for something to move on the face of the waters. Hancock got to his feet, and while he sniffed at the heavily-perfumed flowers he asked:

'What time did this woman first ring up, Ella?'

''Bout half-past two, sir. I was just — er — busy in the kitchen — '

'And at what time did she call personally?'

'About seven o'clock last evening. She thanked me for giving her the address and simply said she wouldn't need to use it after all.'

'Mmmm . . . ' Hancock studied the hyacinths from another angle. 'And what did she look like?'

'I'd say she was about thirty, fairly tall and slim — oh, yes, she had dark hair and was wearing glasses.'

'Dark ones?' Hancock asked.

'No, sir. Thick ones. As though she were shortsighted, or something.'

'And her voice? You say you couldn't be sure on the phone whether she were man or woman. Was there something peculiar in her voice when you met her face to face?'

'No, sir.' Ella gave a shrug. 'I suppose the line must have been bad, or something. She had quite a pleasant voice — same as any woman would have.'

'I'd give something for your geranium beds out there,' Hancock commented, peering through the window on to the front garden. 'Beautifully set out — and healthy, too. How often, if at all, did your master and mistress quarrel, or have a difference of opinion?'

Ella was beginning to show signs of confusion as she tried to sort out the horticulture from the straight questions. With a troubled frown, she answered:

'Practically all the time, sir.'

'Really?' The C.I. turned to look at her, his round face wreathed in its most beaming smile. 'Not what you would call happily married, then?'

'Well — I don't know about that. They argued a lot, but they seemed fond of each other, if you know what I mean. They both seemed pretty angry with each other too, just before they went away. I don't think the master liked the idea of having to go to the cottage — nor could he understand why he had to. At least, that was how it looked to me.'

Hancock mused, his hands deep in his raglan coat pockets.

★   ★   ★

'Ever hear of anybody called Ian, or Mary?' he asked.

Ella thought for a long time, and then shook her head.

'Too bad,' Hancock sighed, and reached for his hat.

'Well, Ella, thanks for everything. You've been quite a help — and by the way . . . '

'Yes, sir?' Ella rose, wide-eyed, expecting some confidential service was going to be asked of her.

'Don't let those geraniums and hyacinths get too dry while the master is away. Flowers feel things you know — just as we do.'

With that Hancock departed, re-entering the police car outside. Grimshaw climbed in beside him, ready to do the driving.

'Anyway, sir, we know we're looking for a woman,' he said.

'I told you that long ago — but whether it's the woman who got so busy yesterday or not I can't be sure. She's got to be checked, though. Tall, dark and slim. Seems to fit Claire Wilton to me. She was at the inquest, of course, but since it was promptly adjourned she would have time to phone here for two-thirty. She must have made up her mind there and then to go to Lancing because she could not have had prior knowledge of the Jackson's departure. What other plan she had which prompted her to ring up, we don't know. Maybe it was just to spy out the lay of the land. Don't forget that Claire said she'd found out all about Vera Bradmore's past life. She may know far more than we ever suspected, otherwise how did she know that Mrs. Elsie Jackson had a tattoo on her back?'

'How about the thick glasses, sir?' Grimshaw asked. 'Was it for disguise?'

Hancock reflected for a moment or two, lighting his evil-smelling pipe.

'Possibly — or there is always the

chance that the woman was not Claire Wilton, but a genuine business caller.'

'Pity she didn't leave her address with Ella,' Grimshaw sighed.

'Well, Ella says she didn't, so that's that . . . just a moment, Harry, before you start driving on to Bloomsbury. I've something I want to work out.'

Hancock pulled a notebook from his pocket and began to figure somewhat laboriously. When he had finished, he looked through the windscreen with narrowed eyes and nodded.

'She could just about do it,' he said, and not having the least idea what his superior was talking about, Grimshaw just gazed at him.

'This woman — if it is Claire Wilton,' Hancock elaborated. 'She phoned about half-past two and got the address. She could have reached Brighton or Worthing in an hour from London here. Reckon another hour before she came upon Elsie Jackson on the beach. That brings us to half-past four. She finished her and caught the first train back. That brings us to, say, half-past six. At seven she called and said she wouldn't bother going to the cottage.'

'But why did she do that?' Grimshaw asked, puzzled.

'To provide an alibi, of course — to convey the impression she had never left London. Quite a neat dodge when you come to think of it. What she overlooks is that we can check up the time and prove that there was a long enough interval for her to commit the crime and get back. It may be one of those false moves that a criminal always makes, and if so we're well away. Anyway, get this damned thing moving to Bloomsbury and let's see what we can find out.'

Grimshaw nodded and pressed the self-starter. When they arrived at the boarding house in Conway Avenue, Bloomsbury, where Claire had her flat, it was the same hard-faced landlady who opened the door. Recognizing the police again, she took care to be respectful.

'Miss Wilton at home?' Hancock asked pleasantly, raising his hat and beaming.

'No, Inspector, I'm afraid she isn't. Matter of fact she's left.'

'Left?' Hancock's eyes sharpened. 'You mean — for good?'

The woman folded her bony arms and nodded. 'For good — yes. She went yesterday evening with all her bags packed, paid up her rent to date — and that was that.'

'But didn't she leave a forwarding address?

'Not a thing. I asked her where I could send mail if there was any, but she said nothing would be coming.'

Hancock thought for a moment and then asked a question:

'Do you happen to know if she had any friends who might know her new address?'

'Not that I know of, Inspector. I never saw her bring anybody home, and nobody ever seemed to call. She kept very much to herself, perhaps because my rules regarding the flats are rather on the strict side.'

'Mmmm — very possibly. Thanks very much all the same.' Obviously irritated, Hancock returned to the car with Grimshaw behind him.

'Blast!' Hancock said, as he settled himself beside the steering wheel. 'Though if she's the guilty party I couldn't expect much else, I suppose.'

'She must be a fool to take such a risk, sir. There doesn't seem to be any doubt any more but what she's the one we want. She created that rather vague alibi by going to the Jackson home — then she cleared. She can be found, though.'

'You bet she can!' Hancock declared. 'I'll circulate her description through the *Police Gazette* the moment I get back to the office. Just the same,' he finished, musing, 'I am a bit puzzled, Harry. She had a good reason for wanting to get her own back on Vera Bradmore, but I can't imagine why she should want to rub out Elsie Jackson as well.'

'Because they were twin sisters, probably,' Grimshaw said. 'I'm sure they must be. No two could be so identical and still be unrelated, in spite of the puzzle of different surnames and the fact that neither ever mentioned the other.'

'And each with a tattoo . . . ' Hancock sat musing, his pipe now extinguished.

' 'Mary' and 'Ian.' What the hell am I supposed to make of that? Anyway, get back to the Yard and I'll get that description circular out — then I'm going to tackle the birth records department and see if I can improve on Davidson's discoveries. Why the deuce the Ministry of Births is still in the northwest of England, where it went during the war, I don't know. Have to phone them, that's all, same as Davidson did.'

Grimshaw nodded and got the car on its way again. It was close on noon when they reached Whitehall once more. They dropped in at a café for lunch and then went on to the smoky little office overlooking the Embankment. Within half-an-hour Hancock had transmitted all the details concerning Claire Wilton to the relevant department. Wherever she was she would be found, and a watch would be placed on all railway and bus stations and air and seaports. With this task out of the way, Hancock turned his attention to the telephone, and his official position gave him a free line to the birth records department in the northwest of England.

'Here's the situation,' he explained in his bland fashion. 'I have all details concerning one Vera Bradmore, whose murder I am investigating, and I know she was the daughter of Arthur Bradmore and Miriam Hilda Bradmore, fairground employees — but I have reason for thinking there was not that one daughter, but two. A twin, in fact. What would the procedure be in that case? Would both births be separately recorded on the same certificate, or what?'

'Separately,' the distant voice answered. 'They are distinct people if not joined to each other by some physical process, and therefore legally entitled to a certificate.'

'Good!' A gleam came into Hancock's eyes. 'That possibly explains how Divisional Inspector Davidson of Kensington, when he was in touch with you recently concerning Vera Bradmore, got no further than her. He had no need to, not suspecting a sister even existed. All right, then, what I want to know is: Is there a record of any other child under the

Bradmore name?'

'I'll have a search made, Inspector, and ring you back.'

'Okay.' Hancock sat back in his chair and rubbed his hands gently together. Grimshaw, who had gathered enough from the conversation to realize what was transpiring, nodded in satisfaction.

'Looks as if we might be getting somewhere, sir,' he commented.

'No doubt of it, my boy.' Hancock sat frowning for a moment, chewing the stem of his extinguished pipe. 'Y'know,' he said slowly, 'I've heard something somewhere connected with the name Bradmore . . . if only I could think what it is! I know it's important, but it keeps on escaping me. I've seen something where the name figures. Must be getting old, I'm afraid. My memory gets worse every day.'

'Can't say it rings a bell for me, sir,' Grimshaw said, after thinking for a while. 'It's not a particularly unusual name, after all. Must be thousands of people with it.'

'Uh-huh . . . ' The Chief Inspector scowled in front of him and remained motionless so long he might have been in a trance. When presently the telephone bell shrilled, he jumped visibly and picked the instrument up. 'Yes. Hancock here.'

In another moment he was speaking to the births registry department again.

'I looked that up for you, Inspector,' came the voice. 'There is Vera Bradmore, of course — as you said — and also Elsie Bradmore, of the same parents, on the same date — July 10th, 1921.'

'That's it!' Hancock banged his fist exultantly on the desk. 'You've made me feel ten years younger — '

'There's another one yet, Inspector,' the voice interrupted.

'Huh? Another one? How do you mean?'

'There's also Janice Bradmore, again of the same parents on the same date.'

Hancock stared in front of him blankly. 'You — you mean there were triplets?' be demanded.

'That's the way it looks, sir.'

'Er — hold on a minute . . . ' Hancock put his hand over the mouthpiece and sat thinking swiftly, his lips compressed; then he said, 'Have the marriage records searched and see if you can find one where the maiden name of the wife is Janice Bradmore. I know it's a tough assignment, but do your best.'

'I'll try, Inspector, and ring you back.'

Hancock put the telephone down again and gazed at Grimshaw across the desk. He paused in 'decoding' his notes to the noiseless typewriter.

'Three of 'em, eh?' he asked. 'Is that a help or a hindrance?'

'Both, my lad, if you ask me. It's a hindrance in so far that if we don't locate this third sister in time she may suffer the fate of the other two; and it's a help because it makes it clear why 'Mary' and 'Ian' don't make sense.' Grimshaw looked puzzled, so Hancock added, 'Don't you see? There may be a third tattoo on this sister Janice which will make the other two make sense . . . or am I crazy?'

He lit his pipe and puffed at it savagely. After a while he said:

'It begins to look as though these three sisters — of whom only Vera Bradmore retained her legal name, and even she disguised it under Madame Luchaire — made some kind of pact to disavow each other, Elsie changing her maiden name to Cartwright, and Janice perhaps changing her name too. If that should prove to be the case, we'll have the devil of a job trying to find her.'

'I just don't understand the set-up,' Grimshaw muttered, rubbing his chin. 'It's very plain that Mrs. Jackson knew her life was in danger, which fact she presumably deduced from seeing the report of her sister's murder — Vera, I mean. Why, then, did she fly off to her beach cottage and try and hide herself? It would have been far easier to come to us, wouldn't it? Or at any rate ask for police protection.'

'Easier, yes,' Hancock admitted, 'but perhaps not desirable. The inference is that there's something strange in the lives of those three women — strange enough to prevent them seeking police aid. Apparently — as far as Elsie Jackson was concerned anyway — they prefer to risk being bumped off first.'

'It mustn't happen to the third sister!'

Grimshaw declared. 'We've just got to find her, sir, and give protection — if only for our reputation's sake.'

'Think I don't know that?' Hancock gave a troubled smile. 'What are you worrying about? I'm the one who'll have to answer to the Assistant Commissioner if anything more goes wrong — not you. I'm expecting him to send for me every minute to find out how far I've got.'

He glanced up as a clerk entered. He came to the desk and put an envelope upon it.

'Medical report and fingerprint findings for Mrs. Elsie Jackson, sir,' he said briefly. 'Just come through.'

'Thanks.' Hancock slit the envelope and took out the broad quarto sheets and batch of photographs. With Grimshaw looking over his shoulder, he studied everything carefully, then finally sat back with a sigh.

'Some good that does us!' he complained. 'She died of asphyxia — which fact we already know — and there are signs of what the doc calls 'manual manipulation' on the back of the neck. In other words, the killer shoved Elsie's face in the wet sand and stifled her. But the bruise marks don't tell much: not a sign of identifiable prints. Gloves may be the answer to that one. So, apparently, we are still no nearer. What exasperates me about this damned business is that the killer behaves with perfect simplicity, and yet for that very reason covers every track.'

Grimshaw nodded moodily and sorted through the photographs which had been taken on the beach where lay the murdered woman's body. After studying a close-up of the tattooed name for a moment, he asked a question.

'I suppose that this 'Ian' tattoo, like the other one on Vera Bradmore, was made in childhood?'

Hancock looked again at the Divisional Surgeon's long report and then nodded.

'Correct, Harry. He mentions it here in a footnote. An identical case to Vera Bradmore — 'Scuse me,' he broke off, and swung round to the telephone as it shrilled. 'Yes? Inspector Hancock here — '

'Oh, hello, Billy! Tom Cavendish here . . . '

Hancock relaxed and grinned. 'You again, eh Tom? Sorry — I thought you were a civil servant with some news for me — No, no, the polite kind,' he added, as Tom Cavendish remonstrated. 'Well, what's on your mind?'

'You are,' the exporter answered. 'What about that visit you were going to make?'

'Waiting for a chance,' Hancock said, realizing that owing to absence of news in the papers, Cavendish had no idea of how the Vera Bradmore case had extended into fresh fields.

'Well, I rang you because I look like having to hop up and down the country a lot in the next few weeks,' Cavendish explained. 'Once that happens our hopes of getting together may be blown sky-high. Like yesterday, for instance, when I had to spend all day in a benighted spot on the south coast.'

'Did you?' Hancock asked vaguely, something turning over in his mind.

'There are drawbacks to being in the exporting job,' Tom Cavendish assured him. 'Tomorrow I'm liable to hop up north again — but tonight I'm free. How about it? I've told the wife and she's itching to meet you.'

'Nice of her,' Hancock chuckled. 'Just the same, I don't see how — '

'Oh, dammit, man, you're not chained body and soul to that confounded job of yours, are you? We've a lot to talk over, you know. The relaxation would do you good. Incidentally, I've got some Napoleon brandy in — the sort, you used to like, and I suppose you still do.'

'That does it!' Hancock declared. 'I'll be there if it kills me. Nothing at the moment that can't wait — but if something very important should crop up and I fail to arrive you'll just have to forgive me. Sometimes things move fast around here . . . otherwise expect me at eight o'clock.'

'Good! I'll look forward to it.'

Hancock put the phone back on its cradle and lay back again in his chair. He caught Sergeant Grimshaw's eye.

'Tom Cavendish,' the Chief Inspector explained. 'One of my best friends. Remember him?'

'Why, yes! Some years ago.'

'He's been abroad and come back with a wife and a comfortable job.' Hancock pulled out his penknife and scraped in the bowl of his pipe, his light eyes fixed absently into distance. 'I suppose I haven't really got the time for a social call,' he said, 'but maybe I should make it . . . Funny thing — Tom Cavendish was doing some business on the south coast yesterday.'

Grimshaw stopped typing and looked up. Then Hancock grinned widely.

'So were lots of other people probably,' he chuckled. 'I'm getting so that I suspect everything and everybody, even my best friend! And that's a bad habit. Funny,' he concluded, his smile fading, 'what coincidence can make you think sometimes.'

'Coincidence?' Grimshaw repeated, struggling to think the matter out.

'Uh-huh. On the night Vera Bradmore was murdered Tom Cavendish was up north seeing some business friends, or something . . . ' Hancock's slowly broadening grin showed how much he disbelieved his own conclusions. 'What am I talking about?' he asked.

'Seems like you're trying to pin something on Tom Cavendish,' Grimshaw told him, who took everything seriously. 'Only it's so ridiculous — just jumping to conclusions. What on earth should he want to kill two women for? Besides, you've decided on a woman.'

'Course I have,' the Chief Inspector agreed, lighting his pipe. 'I'm just fooling. Surprising, when you're in a corner, what sort of angles you think up and the amazing number of people you suspect.' He leaned forward on the desk, puffing gently. 'There's a parallel, though,' he added, musing. 'I once knew a chap who was a double-dyed murderer. In the normal way he was a good friend of mine. It was when he became suddenly anxious to know me better that I began to suspect things. I realized it could not be for my beauty or old-world charm. Later I found the reason.'

'Which was?' Grimshaw asked, interested.

'He had that one thing all killers have — an insatiable vanity. He was so pleased with having fooled the police he couldn't resist the temptation to be friendly with the chief investigator — myself. He wanted to watch me make mistakes at close quarters and chuckle over his superiority. He over-reached himself, though. I got him in the end.'

There was silence for a moment. The smile had gone from Hancock's face now. His pale eyes were fixed on distance as the smoke curled pungently from his pipe. Then Grimshaw made an observation:

'You can't seriously mean you suspect Mr. Cavendish, sir?'

'Course I don't.' Hancock gave a start and beamed. 'Just drawing parallels, as I told you. I could say that he's renewed an old friendship to find out how far I've got; I could say that he is back of everything if his visits to north and south respectively can't be proved ... but without a shred of evidence for thinking such things, the A.C. would justifiably kick me out on my behind and I'd deserve it. That's the worst of this business, Harry; you get to thinking things. I'll even start suspecting myself if I don't make a change

— plant some seeds, prune the rose-bushes, or something — '

'Something occurs to me,' Grimshaw said, considering his notes again. 'I thought Derek Cantrill said he thought he might be able to prove his alibi. He didn't at the inquest. Told the same story as before. Any idea what he could have meant?'

'A very good idea,' Hancock said dryly. 'He probably thought he could bribe somebody to get him out of the mess, and that somebody wouldn't have any. It's done thousands of times and we can't always pin it down. That's why I say an inquest should, wherever practicable, be held immediately. The doubtful ones get too much leeway to sort themselves out, which hampers us. In any case, I'm not bothering much about Cantrill. I dislike him personally, but I don't think he had anything to do with the murders — chiefly because I've had tabs on him. Reports show that after the inquest yesterday he went straight back to his office — so he couldn't have done anything on the south coast, could he?'

'Seems to let him out,' Grimshaw admitted. 'But if you had tabs on him, why not on Claire Wilton? She's got clean away with it.'

'I didn't watch everybody,' Hancock said moodily. 'It would have been an almost impossible task with a limited number of men at my disposal. I only concentrated on Cantrill because, up to yesterday, he struck me as a likely one to make false moves. Now, I've had my nose punched I know better — though, somehow, I still cannot think of Claire Wilton as a sadistic killer.'

'Can't judge by appearances in our business, sir,' Grimshaw commented heavily.

'How right you are — ' Hancock lifted the telephone as it rang. 'Hancock here. Yes? Oh — yes . . . ' He sat listening. 'Tomorrow at ten. Okay, I'll he there. After that Jackson can be allowed to come back home if he wants. Yes — goodbye.'

The telephone went back on its rest and Hancock added, 'The inquest's at Worthing tomorrow. That was Superintendent Baines. He says they haven't found any signs of footprints anywhere on the sands. Which, I'm afraid, can be explained by the killer smoothing them out as she — or he — progressed. Easy to do in sand. Even the wind might have done it.'

Again the telephone rang. He lifted it languidly. 'Hancock here. Yes?'

It was the department for births and marriages again.

'Sorry, Inspector, but as far as we can tell there doesn't seem to he any sign of a marriage recorded under the name of Janice Bradmore.'

'I expected it,' Hancock sighed. 'For that matter I don't even know if she is married. May even be dead for all I know to the contrary. You'd better see if there's anything in the deaths and ring me back.'

'Okay, Inspector; I'll do that.'

Hancock put the phone back and mused. 'This,' he confessed, 'is like the needle in the haystack. Unless Janice Bradmore — or whoever she is now — comes forward when she sees from the papers what is happening, I don't know how we can find her, granting she is alive.

Might put out a request through the press for her to communicate with us — though I hardly think she will if she's no more communicative than her unfortunate sisters.'

Grimshaw nodded thoughtfully, but said nothing.

'Bradmore,' the Chief Inspector muttered, frowning. 'I know I've heard that name somewhere! Gosh almighty, if only my memory would do its stuff, I could take a giant's stride. Have to go on thinking; mebby it will come back to me.'

'You mean, sir, the ban on information to the press will be lifted?' Grimshaw asked.

'After the inquest tomorrow it will have to be. Can't keep it dark any longer then. Maybe it will help if we do give some news; might start the killer off on a fresh tack and so help us.'

7

At eight o'clock that evening, in accordance with his promise, Hancock arrived at the Wimbledon home of Tom Cavendish. It proved to be a sizeable modern villa, detached from its immediate neighbors. It had a comfortable, if not a moneyed appearance.

Cavendish himself opened the door — tall, bronzed, and smiling. The greetings over and his hat and coat on a peg on the hallstand, Hancock found himself led into a wide, comfortable lounge. A youngish woman, who had apparently been busy stirring the fire into some life — for the late evening was decidedly chilly — hung up the poker carefully on its stand and came over quickly.

'Here she is, Billy,' Tom Cavendish said with a smile. 'Betty! This is Billy Hancock, Betty.'

'Of Scotland Yard,' Betty added, laughing. 'You forgot that bit, Tom. How are you, Mr. Hancock? I really am glad to meet you.'

She shook hands warmly as Hancock gave his broad, indulgent grin. Betty Cavendish was slim, straight, and tallish, with youthful strength in every line of her figure. She had quick gray eyes, a wide mouth, and somewhat tumbled fair hair. She was not exactly pretty, a deficiency which had compensation in her charm of manner.

'Call me Billy.' Hancock smiled. 'Tom does, so you certainly must. I'm called other things too,' he added dryly.

In a few moments the inevitable stiffness of first introduction had eased and the three were seated around the crackling fire. Hancock looked blissfully content, a glass of Napoleon brandy on the occasional table near him. His pipe crackled noisily while Betty and her husband smoked cigarettes.

'Obviously,' Hancock said, spreading his hands, 'I don't need to ask if you're both happy? I never saw a married couple looking so pleased with themselves.'

'Ideally happy,' Betty agreed, with a

fond glance at her husband's handsome face. 'We've been married over a year now and the — the effect,' — she laughed gaily at her choice of words — 'doesn't seem to have worn off any. Does it, Tom?'

'Wonder it doesn't, though,' he said. 'I'm away such a lot, it's a mystery to me how you can put up with it. I hate leaving you alone so many hours, and sometimes days, at a stretch.'

'Don't you worry, darling,' Betty patted his knee solemnly as he sat beside her. 'If you didn't go about your business a fine old mess we'd be in.'

'Just what do you do on these perambulations of yours?' Hancock enquired; and Tom Cavendish gave a shrug.

'I'm with Bolton's, the big agricultural engineers,' he explained. 'Their headquarters are in London here, but they have a lot of branches scattered up and down the country — subsidiary engineering shops. Different machinery in each one. If I have a big export order to handle it demands that I go tearing up and down to the different branches to get what I want. If things were, decentralized — a system which began during the war when the bombing was severe — it would help me a lot.'

'Uh-huh . . . ' Hancock drew at his pipe, his eyes moving from Tom Cavendish to Betty, then back to Tom again.

'That's enough about engineering,' Betty decided suddenly. 'What about you, Billy? Your job intrigues me, you know.'

'So Tom told me.' Hancock passed a hand over his convict's haircut. 'Hanged if I know why. I can't think of anything less romantic than Scotland Yard.'

'But it is — to the outsider. For instance . . . ' Betty hunched forward eagerly in the armchair, her gray eyes bright. 'This tattoo business you're working on. It must be fascinating.'

'It's grim, Betty — infernally grim. I'd much sooner be potting out tomato slips in my own greenhouse. I think if I didn't have my gardening for a hobby, I'd go crazy. My business is a beastly one, and don't you forget it.'

'Anyway, you haven't come to talk shop,' Tom said, smiling.

'I know, but . . . ' Betty hesitated. 'I just happen to be interested in crime, that's all. Look over there,' she added, and motioned to a tall bookcase well filled with crime novels by celebrated authors.

Hancock chuckled. 'You may be interested in it, Betty, but I can't tell you much about it. I'm bound by secrecy — so let's forget all about it, shall we? By the way, I don't quite get your accent. Are you English?'

'English as you are,' she laughed. 'I was born in London here.'

'Oh, really? I thought I detected a faint American twang.'

'That's with my living abroad so long,' Betty said, smiling. 'I was in America when I met Tom.'

'Right,' he confirmed. 'And it struck me when I walked into one of the big American engineering firms one day that the secretary to the big shot was just the girl I wanted. So that's what happened. Betty felt the same way, and there we were.'

'So Betty Dyson became Betty Cavendish,' Hancock chuckled, and inspected his pipe, thoughtfully.

'How — did you know about her maiden name'?' Tom Cavendish asked, frowning. 'I don't recall I ever mentioned it.'

'You didn't,' Hancock assured him. 'But on the mantel shelf there I notice there are three silver trophy cups — one for long-distance swimming, another for the high jump, and a third for the hundred yards sprint, all awarded to Betty Dyson. Simple, isn't it?'

Betty smiled. 'Good as Sherlock Holmes himself,' she agreed. 'I'm proud of those cups,' she added, glancing up at them. 'When I was younger, I loved athletics of any sort.'

'So Tom mentioned. He's been extolling your virtues quite a lot, believe me. Not that you're so old now,' Hancock said, refilling his pipe. 'Not a day over twenty-eight, I'd say.'

'Thirty in August. Heading for the danger line.'

For a moment or two the conversation drifted variously over sports, weather, and football pools — then Hancock came back to a question with the suddenness peculiar to him.

'By the way, Tom, did you say you were up north on the night Vera Bradmore got herself strangled?'

'Vera Bradmore?' Tom repeated vaguely; then he seemed to remember. 'Oh, the woman with the tattoo! Yes — I'd been up to Manchester. Betty gave me the news about the murder when I landed home here about half-past eight in the morning . . . seems to me I told you that before at the club.'

'Uh-huh. And yesterday you were down at the south coast, I think you said?'

'That's right. I had some business at a shadow factory in Eastbourne.'

There was silence for a moment, both Tom and the girl gazing in obvious surprise. Hancock saw their looks and chuckled.

'Good job you're not involved in this murder business,' he said dryly. 'As an example, Betty — since you love crime puzzles — I might have to run your dearly beloved husband in on suspicion if he couldn't prove his movements.'

'But I can!' Tom protested. 'What in blazes are you talking about?'

'Just stating a theoretical case for your entertainment. Police reasoning would be this: You, Tom, were absent on business — allegedly — when Vera Bradmore was murdered. You were again absent at the time her sister, Elsie Jackson, was murdered — on the south coast, yesterday! Sheer coincidence, of course, but you see what I mean.'

'It's fascinating!' Betty declared, intensely interested; then she frowned, 'You mean there's been a second murder? I haven't heard about it.'

'You will — after the inquest tomorrow. So will everybody else.' Hancock gave the details in so far as he thought necessary, and when he had finished, Betty looked at her husband.

'Going to keep you busy, Betty, watching all the moves,' he commented, smiling. 'And I'm liable to have the details related to me every time I'm at home, Billy.'

'Wish I could tell you more,' Hancock said, 'but officialdom prevents me . . . and there I go! I wasn't going to talk shop, yet here I am on the job whether I intended to or not. Old habits die hard, I suppose.'

'I think,' Betty said, getting to her feet, 'that it's time we had some refreshment — if you'll pardon me. I've got everything ready.'

She left the room with a lithe grace and the door closed. Hancock relaxed in his chair, studying Tom Cavendish's handsome face through the smoke from his pipe.

'Like my choice?' Tom asked.

'Perfect.'

'Look . . . ' A frown crossed Tom's forehead. 'You don't really mean you think I'm mixed up in this horrible business, do you?'

'Course not,' Hancock grinned. 'Just pulling your leg. I often do it; I enjoy watching the victims' faces.'

'Seems rather a cruel sense of humor to me. I never thought you were that kind of man.'

'I've always been an odd egg, as the saying is. But ask yourself a question: why on earth should I suspect you of being mixed up in this mystery?'

'I dunno. Just the way you talked. If you like I can tell you where I was when these things happened — '

'Great heavens, no,' Hancock laughed; then he glanced up as Betty returned, pushing a tea trolley loaded with refreshments. For the time being the subject of murder investigation was dropped and Hancock took care that he did not refer to it again. Instead the conversation turned on commonplaces, and remained that way until, towards ten o'clock, Hancock glanced up at the big clock on the mantle.

'Well, have to be going,' he sighed. 'I've a busy day before me tomorrow — and the wife will want to talk when I get home, I suppose. Her privilege.'

He got to his feet, shaking the creases out of his untidy suit and pushing his pipe into his pocket.

'I've had a grand time,' he said. 'Been just like it used to be, Tom. Have to see if we can't make it stay that way. I'd like you and the wife to come over to my place one of these evenings — when I'm

149

clear of this present investigation, that is.'

'Glad to,' Tom said, smiling. 'Not that I can do it in the next fortnight, though. As I told you I've a lot of rushing about to do to these various branches — tomorrow I'm off again for three or four days.'

'Good job I trust him, isn't it?' Betty asked archly.

Hancock chuckled and ambled his way into the hall. In five more minutes he was on his way through the cold, May dusk, thinking on many things as he walked. To his wife, as ever, he said but little regarding his professional activities; they had a tacit agreement that his work finished when he left Whitehall for the day.

Next morning, however, Sergeant Grimshaw was not so easily satisfied. The moment he had greeted his chief he asked a straight-to-the-point question.

'Well, sir, did you see Mr. Cavendish and his wife last night?'

'Uh-huh. Had a nice time, too. She's quite a charming girl.' Hancock seated himself at the desk and contemplated the morning correspondence set out in orderly piles.

'I mean . . . did you substantiate anything, sir? You had a theory yesterday — sort of, anyway.'

'Oh, that?' Hancock grinned and lighted his pipe. 'Just a bit of idle reflection, Harry. Certainly nothing happened last evening to start me thinking. I could suspect Tom Cavendish if I wanted, of course, so maybe the best way to cure myself of that is to test his alibis at the times of the two recent murders. Tell you what you might do: ring up Bolton's, the agricultural engineers, in Manchester and Eastbourne, and find out if Tom was visiting them about the time we know the murders were committed. If he was, then that settles it. He has nothing to do with it.'

'Then you do feel he might he implicated?' Grimshaw asked, raising the telephone.

'Well, I . . . ' Hancock hesitated, scowling at his pipe in his hand. 'Y'see, Harry, I still can't understand why Tom has gone out of his way so persistently to make me visit him. It doesn't somehow . . . ring true. The way it looks, he only started to hunt me up when he knew I was on the Bradmore case, and since then he's hardly left me alone. Maybe quite natural, maybe not. We were good friends, but not intimate ones. I just don't get it.'

'Did you get the idea last night that he was trying to pump you to see how far you'd got?'

'They both did,' Hancock answered. 'But it looked like idle curiosity. Anyway, see if you can find out anything and let me get this damnable bee out of my bonnet. Things have come to a fine pass when I start suspecting my own friends without a shred of reason for doing it.'

Grimshaw lifted the telephone and, with the usual diplomatic skill which he exercised over such matters — never for a moment admitting he was a police officer — he contacted both Manchester and Eastbourne and talked for quite a while. Hancock, listening as he smoked, gathered enough to know the answers by the time the sergeant had finished.

'Everything okay, sir,' Grimshaw said. 'Mr. Cavendish was at one or other place at the approximate times of the murders.

So that lets him out.'

'Thank goodness,' Hancock said. 'That's one worry I can chuck overboard.' He examined the correspondence and reports on the desk. 'Nothing yet concerning Claire Wilton, I notice.'

'Not yet, sir.'

'And judging from this report here from Robertson, Derek Cantrill doesn't seem to be doing anything at all suspicious. I think we can knock him off our list, too. More one considers this, the more Claire Wilton seems to fill the bill — especially the way she's walked off.'

'I myself don't trust George Jackson too much,' Grimshaw said, thinking. 'It's a rotten alibi to say you're asleep when a murder happens. Surely he would have heard something?'

'Not if he sleeps like I do,' Hancock grinned. 'Take an atom bomb to shift me. Anyway, we can't waste time sitting here. We've that inquest to attend in Worthing, so we'd better be going. Maybe we'll get something out of it.'

'There's this, too, sir,' Grimshaw said,

as Hancock rose. 'About Janice Bradmore's death — no sign of anything under that name. Registry phoned through just before you came this morning.'

'Like I said — a needle in a haystack,' the Chief Inspector sighed. 'Well — come on.'

But the inquest, which Hancock had adjourned pending further enquiry, did not add anything to his information. George Jackson clung to his original statement and so, for that matter, did the maid Ella, who had been summoned to give her side of the matter.

'*Ex nihilo nihil fit*,' Hancock commented, as he and Grimshaw sat in the train on the return journey to London. '' Out of nothing, nothing comes.' Very soon the Assistant Commissioner is going to start saying rude things to me. I — '

He stopped dead, staring blankly through the window on to the flying countryside. Grimshaw raised an enquiring eyebrow.

'Harry, I've got it!' Hancock breathed, clenching his fist. He turned, his pale eyes bright. 'I've just remembered where I've heard the name 'Bradmore' before. Or rather seen it. It was in the Criminal Records Office. You remember the Brayford case, which we've just finished?'

'Yes, sir. I was typing out the final details on it when the Divisional Inspector dumped the Bradmore business in your lap.'

'Correct. Well, the Brayford case necessitated me looking through the C.R.O. files and that was where I noticed Bradmore — in the same index shelf. I remember it now! Sooner I get back and look again the better I'll like it. If I don't knock some sense into this case soon I'll go crazy'

★   ★   ★

News of the second 'Tattoo Murder,' as the mysterious business of the slain women had now been called, traveled far faster than Hancock or Grimshaw, with the result that by the time they had reached London again the news was already on the streets in the early evening editions.

Not that Hancock was interested; he had his mind fixed on investigating the files in C.R.O. But a fashionably dressed youngish woman seated in a sleek Rolls-Royce became suddenly alert as the strident voice of a newsboy drifted to her.

'Second murder! 'Nother tattoo mystery! First edishun!'

Janice Mottram, the third triplet, her features and figure identical to the two women who had already died, lowered the window of the car, holding her handkerchief partly to her face as she did so.

'Boy!' she called. 'Here, boy — a paper, please.'

'Right y'are, lady — ' the boy came whizzing up, took no more than a passing glance at her half-shielded features, then went on his way bawling his wares.

Janice sank back in the cushions, reading the stop-press details. She had come to an end of them when Barrington, her chauffeur, reappeared from the store where he had been making purchases. He placed them on the seat beside him, then settled at the wheel.

156

'Home, Barrington, please,' Janice requested.

'But, madam, I thought you said you wished to call on — '

'Never mind that. Take me home.'

'Very good.'

Barrington was too well trained to ask questions. In fact he hardly needed to. He knew already, from his own observations, that his mistress was astoundingly like the dead Vera Bradmore; and he had also heard the newsboy shouting about a second tattoo murder. Probably it added up. Barrington was not concerned whether it did or not. He was well paid, had a comfortable situation, and cared nothing for the private life of his employers.

Once she was within the safety of 'The Larches,' Maida Vale, Janice seemed to lose something of her ill-controlled agitation; but she was still not settled enough to concentrate upon anything particular. It was a mood of intense uneasiness that lasted until her husband, Richard, came home towards six o'clock. The moment he entered the big drawing room he could sense her disquiet.

'Anything wrong, dear?' he asked in concern. Indeed Janice was his only idol. He was some fifteen years older than she, a fact that lent to him a kind of paternal interest in all her activities. Smiling, kindly, she had never had reason to regret the moment she had married him.

'Everything, Dick,' she answered, and faced him seriously.

'Oh, come now . . . ' His placid, rather pink face — rendered more so by the gray of his hair at the temples, showed that he considered her worry needless. 'Whatever it is we can soon sort it out. What is it? Money?'

'As if it could be,' she sighed. Money she had in plenty. Richard Mottram was one of the city's wealthiest perfumiers. 'It's something . . . horrifying. Something I've always kept to myself — but I can't do it any longer. I've got to tell somebody.'

'Oh?' He considered her with surprised blue eyes. 'You mean some kind of illness?'

'No . . . it concerns — murder.'

Richard Mottram was too mature to start — but he did go across to the door, open it, and look out into the hall. Satisfied, he closed the door again and came over to take Janice's arm, motioning to the settee.

'Sit down, my dear, and tell me all about it. We have time before dinner.'

He settled opposite her and waited. Janice hesitated as she tried to find a suitable way to begin.

'You are aware, Dick, that I have a tattoo on my back,' she said.

'Of course, Jan. It spells L-I-L, doesn't it?'

'Yes. I — I never intended really that you should see it. You wouldn't have, either, but for my swimsuit getting ripped on that rock last summer.'

He laughed softly. 'Well, that isn't a tragedy, is it? In fact I should think you are the one to be discomfited. It spoils you for these fashionable low-cuts, doesn't it?'

'That tattoo means something, Dick. Not of itself, but tied up with two other tattoos.'

He was silent, frowning and trying not to look bewildered.

'You must have heard of the 'Tattoo Murders',' Janice said urgently. 'First it was Vera Bradmore, of Kensington, and now Elsie Jackson, who was murdered two days ago on the beach near Lancing.'

'I rarely read the papers, as you know,' her husband said, 'but now you mention it, I do recall something — why, of course! I remarked on the likeness of that woman Vera Bradmore to you when I saw her photograph in the paper.'

'That's right; and I stopped you reading further in case you saw that she had a tattoo on her back. That would have made you think things about me since I've a tattoo also.'

'Yes,' Richard Mottram admitted; 'I probably would have been a bit puzzled. However, I didn't bother reading about it — but what is it all about anyway?'

'Vera Bradmore and Elsie Jackson were my sisters,' Janice stated deliberately. 'We were triplets.'

'Vera Bradmore was unmarried,' Richard pointed out. 'I did notice that much. That being so, your maiden name should have been Bradmore too — but on the marriage license you gave it as 'Crawford,' under which name I knew you before we married.'

'It was assumed,' Janice sighed. 'So was Elsie's maiden name. We both deliberately changed our maiden names. Only Vera kept hers correct.'

Richard spread his hands. 'Forgive me, Jan, but I just can't make out what you're getting at. You say these two women were your sisters — I haven't seen anything about the second one — this — er — Elsie Jackson.'

'It's in the stop press tonight — just announced. That was why I wanted to talk to you about it. Otherwise you'd certainly have questioned me because of my resemblance to the two women. We made a pact never to communicate with each other unless great urgency demanded it. That was because of the tattoos on our backs. We never had the tattoos removed because we didn't want

161

anybody to know about them.'

'Why not?' Richard frowned deeply. 'What's it all about?'

Janice got up restlessly from the settee and looked down at her husband with troubled eyes.

'If I were to tell you there'd be the most horrible scandal when the news got out,' she said. 'And it would get out. The public, to say nothing of the police, are desperately anxious for every scrap of news concerning these tattoo murders. I could tell them everything — but I don't intend to.'

'I'm not sure that you're being very sensible, dear,' Richard commented, getting on his feet. 'In fact it's your duty to explain matters. These two unhappy women were your sisters, you say? Doesn't it mean something to you that you can put their murderer behind bars?'

'I don't know that I can, Dick. I've no real idea who the killer is.'

'But you just said — '

'I said I could explain the tattoos, not identify the murderer. If I explained the tattoos it would mean that you in your high social position and I as your wife, would be very much degraded. I love you too much to bring that about, so I don't intend to tell the police anything . . . I do believe, though, that my own life is now in danger.'

'Why?' Richard asked, with quiet grimness. 'Because you too have a tattooed back?'

'Yes. I'm quite certain that these murders have only been committed so that the killer can see the tattoos. The reason for the killing is to prevent anything being given away afterwards as to the murderer's identity.'

'Great heavens, Jan, what kind of a man do you think I am? With a threat like this hanging over you do you expect me to let things be and not tell the police anything? I'm going to this minute — and demand protection for you.'

'If you do that, it's possible that the murderer of my two sisters will never be found,' Janice said quietly.

'Why do you say that?'

'Because the killer will know I am protected by the police. That sort of information can't be kept quiet from the newspapers. Since I am the last integral link in this chain of murders, the killer will lie low if I am guarded — and it is quite plain that so far the police haven't much idea who is responsible. The whole case would fall to pieces because the last link would not be complete and the killer would not strike again. But once police protection was removed, as it would have to be finally, I'd be struck down instantly.'

Richard dug his hands in his coat pockets and mooched pensively about the drawing room.

'This is an appalling situation,' he muttered. 'The way you put it, it sounds as though you want to put yourself in the line of fire so the killer can be drawn into the open!'

'I do,' Janice answered simply. 'There's no other way, as far as I can see, and I owe it to my sisters to avenge them.'

'But surely, if you told the police, they would see to it that no clue got out? They would let you carry out your plan, but would still guard you. They have the power to ask the press to keep quiet on certain details if necessary.'

'True — but my bringing them into it would involve one or other of them coming here to interview me; or else I might have to go from here to Scotland Yard.'

'What of it?'

'If I am watched by the murderer, as I believe I may be at this very moment, what would he think? Obviously, that I was in touch with the police. No, Dick, I'm not taking that risk. I prefer to work this out in my own way and make sure of nailing the killer, even using myself as the bait.'

'You'd better have a mighty good plan, Jan, before I'll let you play ducks and drakes with your life. You're everything in the world to me, remember.'

'That, dearest, I know only too well.' Janice moved across the room slowly and laid a gentle hand on her husband's arm. 'I think my best method is to let it be known through the society columns of the daily papers that I intend to have a vacation — alone — at our villa in the south of France. Cannes, of course. Say, in two days' time.'

'Simple enough,' Richard agreed. 'The society gossip writers are always glad of news concerning your activities and mine — but how do you know the murderer will know that Mrs. Janice Mottram — or rather Mrs. Richard Mottram — is you? Unless you publish a photograph of yourself.'

'I shan't do that; and never have. The killer will know it is me, I'm convinced, because I believe he — or she — knew everything from the moment he murdered Vera. She must have given all the necessary information; otherwise how could Elsie ever have been found under her married name?'

Richard rubbed his chin pensively. 'Any guarantee the killer will read the society columns?'

'No; but if he's anxious to keep a watch on me I shouldn't think he would neglect the one source where he can possibly learn my future movements. Anyway. I'm banking on it. So then, if it works out that way, I shall reach our villa and there, no doubt, the killer will also turn up, sooner or later.'

'Then?'

'For one thing I shall be armed. You can let me have that small automatic you keep as a precaution against burglary. If I am attacked, I shall hold up the intruder — wound him, if need be, but I'll certainly get him — or her. I don't want to kill because I'd never get the needed confession that way.'

Richard shook his head and sighed. 'My dear girl, you don't suppose a ruthless murderer like this would be afraid of your automatic, do you? He'd probably finish you before you even realized what had happened.'

'Do you think he would if Barrington were on the watch, too? He's a strong man, and completely trustworthy. I can give him orders without him asking the why and wherefore. I would also take Mrs. Bates, our housekeeper. She's square, immovable, and not easily frightened. With two people like that to help me, and myself with a gun, I don't think any intruder would stand a chance. Barrington and Mrs. Bates would go on separately, of course, so as not to have any apparent connection with me. In any case they'll have to go since I can't manage the villa by myself.'

'And I don't enter into it at all?' Richard asked quietly. 'That it? You expect me to allow you to take these fantastic risks?'

Janice nodded seriously. 'I do, yes. If you came with me I'm pretty sure that no attempt would be made to get at me. I have got to be more or less alone — as Vera and Elsie were.'

'I still don't like it. After all, your only objection to telling the police seems to be because they would have to come here or you would have to go to them. Why should that be necessary? You could telephone and keep the thing secret, and they certainly would do likewise once they knew the facts.'

'This,' Janice said, 'is an unusual business. It relies on the fact that I am one of three triplets. Do you think the police would ever believe me without seeing me face to face to verify my resemblance to Elsie and Vera? Of course they wouldn't; we would have to meet

— and I don't intend to. Besides, I would have to explain so many other things I don't wish to.'

'You'll have to in any case if you trap the murderer. Every fact and detail will be sifted.'

'All I can hope for is that the facts will not be too baldly stated. Also, the fact that I brought the killer to justice should of itself mitigate the personal circumstances, and help you maintain your reputation.'

Richard was silent for a moment or two, then he gave a sigh. 'You have a tremendous lot of faith in me, haven't you?' he asked quietly. 'Faith enough indeed to feel sure that I won't try and find out what the mystery is in your life?'

'We trust each other,' Janice replied. 'There can't be any more to say than that. One day I'll tell you all about it, and in the meantime I'm grateful for your understanding.'

Richard gave her a peculiar look that she found hard to interpret.

'Very well,' he said. 'Have it your way

— and you can have that automatic of mine. I still think it's a fantastic risk to take, but I also think that perhaps there is really no other way. Now . . . shall we be preparing for dinner?'

8

'This,' said Chief Inspector Hancock, 'is damned interesting! About the first thing in this whole crazy set-up which makes sense, Harry.'

The sergeant said nothing, contenting himself with a nod. He and his superior were seated at a broad, polished desk in the lengthy, well-lighted vista of the Criminal Records Office of Scotland Yard. Around them were the endless rows of steel filing cabinets, carefully indexed. Above them the electric clock said 5-0. On the desk in front of them was a long index drawer with one card removed. Hancock studied it thoughtfully. It gave a photograph of a youngish, good-looking man with dark hair, together with his fingerprints and case history.

''Arthur Bradmore',' Hancock murmured, repeating the wording of the type-written text. ''Aged thirty-two.

Occupation: Fairground tattooist. Convicted of robbery on September 10th, 1919. Sentenced to one year's hard labor. On June 4th, 1924, was killed while resisting arrest after a diamond robbery, in which jewels to the value of £100,000 were stolen and not recovered. At this time Bradmore's address was 9 Chauncy Street, East Dock, London, E.4'.'

'I begin,' Sergeant Grimshaw said, 'to feel something knocking, sir. Namely, a hundred thousand quid in diamonds. That seems to be the missing link in this whole business. In fact literally, since apparently those diamonds were never found.'

'Uh-huh. Here we have the father of the triplets, two of them having been murdered and the third God knows where. Let's see now . . . The kids were born on — er — ' Hancock fished out his notebook. 'On July 10th, 1921. That means they were three years old when their old man got the works. What happened to them after that? That is what we want to know. You notice something else that is significant, Harry? Arthur Bradmore was a tattooist. It doesn't take genius to appreciate that he was the one who did the tattooing on the baby girls' backs, though why he did it is still as big a mystery as before . . . '

Hancock glanced up as a constable came in. He moved over to the table.

'Sorry to interrupt, sir, but there's a couple of p.c. men in your office. They want to see you. They've picked up a Miss Wilton.'

'I'll come,' Hancock said and left Grimshaw to put the file back in the cabinet. Arriving in his office, Hancock found Claire Wilton, pale and troubled, seated at his desk with the two plain-clothes men on either side of her.

'Evening, sir,' one of them said. 'We picked up Miss Wilton here in a Leeds café, where she'd taken on a job as a waitress, so we brought her right over.'

'Which is a sheer waste of time!' Claire declared hotly. 'I strongly resent this police interference with my liberty, Inspector! After all, I still have rights as a citizen.'

'Of course you have, Miss Wilton . . . '
Hancock settled at his desk and beamed
on her. 'It would have made it simpler,
though, if you had informed me before
departing to Leeds. I would not have
stopped you going — indeed I have no
power to do so — but at least I would
have known where to get in touch with
you.'

Claire Wilton gazed at him angrily and
passed no comment. Hancock jerked his
bullet head slightly and the two plain-
clothes men departed just as Grimshaw
came in. He went silently to his corner
desk to start taking notes.

'Until this case is cleared up, Miss
Wilton, you are liable to questioning at
any moment,' Hancock explained, lighting his pipe. 'Sorry, but that's the way it
is. What suddenly led you to depart for
Leeds?'

'I couldn't stand the atmosphere
around here. I felt that you were likely to
arrest me at any moment for murder —
so I just walked out.'

'Ran for it, you mean?' Hancock smiled
good-humoredly. 'Well. I can't say I

blame you, even if it was foolish. However — you are probably aware by now that a second murder has taken place in Lancing? This time it was a Mrs. Elsie Jackson, who, with Vera Bradmore and another woman we haven't yet traced, comprised one of three identical triplets.'

'I've had no chance to see anything,' Claire answered sullenly. 'I was suddenly arrested by those two men while I was at my job in the café — around noon today — and then I was brought here. If there has been a second murder, I had nothing to do with it, any more than with the first.'

'It happened on the day of the inquest — also the day you disappeared, presumably to Leeds. From you, Miss Wilton, I want a statement of what you did after leaving the inquest.'

'I went straight to Marsden's Garage and spent the afternoon talking to Terry Baxter. I told him I intended clearing out and he said it would be unwise. I was resolved, though, and carried out my intention. Then I went to my flat, got my things together, and left — leaving no forwarding address.'

Hancock drew thoughtfully at his pipe, his pale eyes fixed on the girl's animated face.

'Yes, that checks up,' he agreed. 'We know you left your flat in the early evening. Your landlady said so — but, who is this Terry Baxter chap? A boyfriend?'

'More than that. We hope to be married if I can ever shake free of this horrible business.'

'Presumably he can verify you spent the afternoon talking to him?'

'Most certainly he can. So can other people.' Claire Wilton began to warm up as she evidently saw a chance to prove her actions. 'You see, Terry — that is, Mr. Baxter — is the manager of Marsden's Garage. He has a little glass-walled office in the middle of the garage floor. Lots of mechanics at work saw him and me in conversation if . . . you want to ask them.'

'What time did you arrive at the garage?' Hancock asked.

'About two-twenty. I went straight from the inquest — which you had adjourned

— yes, it was two-twenty. I remember noticing the office clock.'

Hancock passed a hand over his shaven head and regarded a cobweb in a far corner of the ceiling.

'And you left about when?'

'Quarter to five. I went to a café and had some tea — The Golden Grill, a few yards from the garage, and I think the waitress would remember me again; then I went on to my flat, packed, and departed.'

'Mmmm . . . you must have had a lot to say in two and a half hours.'

'I'm afraid we did,' Claire muttered. 'It — it was chiefly argument. Terry said I was a fool to run out, and now I realize he was right. He did all he could to stop me.'

'Wise man, Terry,' Hancock grinned. 'Marsden's Garage, you say? What's their number?'

'Central, four two — ' Claire looked up at the clock. 'If you're ringing up you should about catch Terry in.'

'Just what I thought — get busy, Harry, will you?'

Grimshaw nodded and, as usual,

exerted his solid tact when it came to asking questions. The answers could not be heard in the receiver, but evidently all was well for he nodded when he put the phone back on its cradle.

'Checks, sir — and the mechanics can prove it too. If need be.'

'That won't be necessary,' Hancock said. 'I'm satisfied — and, Miss Wilton, I think you should know that your deciding to visit your boy friend like that has helped you a lot. It has conclusively proved that you were not in any way connected with the case of Mrs. Jackson.'

'That's a relief,' Claire said, her eyes brightening. 'A greater relief than I can ever tell you — but I notice you don't say it disconnects me with the Vera Bradmore case.'

'As far as that is concerned, you still have not given me any really definite alibi . . . However, I should not concern yourself unduly. I shall even permit you to return to your job in Leeds, on the understanding that if you change your address you advise me immediately. That has got to be done. Co-operate with me,

Miss Wilton, and you've nothing to fear. If you obstruct things there'll be trouble. That's the straight issue.'

'I'll do whatever you wish,' Claire promised. 'I can see now that I have been several kinds of a fool. In fact, I don't think I will return to Leeds. I'll stay in London and try and get a small room somewhere while I recover my financial loss. I feel I can't apply for anything in my own line of business with this terrible thing hanging over my head.'

Hancock shrugged. 'Just the way of things, I'm afraid. In any event, keep me in touch with your movements.'

His manner was sufficient to show that the interview was at an end. Claire rose and hesitatingly held out her hand. With a smile Hancock rose and shook it, seeing her to the office door.

'Don't worry too much, Miss Wilton,' he said. 'I'm sure you and this bright boy Terry will start out to rear a happy home before you're finished. I have human interests, you know, even if I am a policeman.'

Claire smiled her gratitude and

departed. Rubbing his scalp, Hancock came back to the desk, then raised an eyebrow.

'Strike her off the list, Harry,' he said briefly. 'It's dead certain she'd nothing to do with the Elsie Jackson murder — so I don't see how she could possibly have had anything to do with the Vera Bradmore one either. Both crimes, it's more or less certain, were committed by the same person — and have some tea sent in, will you?'

It had arrived, and both men were seated at it before Hancock spoke again.

'Point now is: who was the woman who rang up and later called at the Jackson home? I got the idea it might have been Claire wearing thick glasses. That's out. Might have been a genuine business caller, as I said before, or it might have been . . . ' He stopped, thought hard over something, then shook his bullet head to himself. 'The things I think of!' he sighed.

There was silence again for a while as the tea was proceeded with; then Hancock seemed to arrive at a decision.

'Tomorrow, Harry, we start off on a

fresh track. We're going to see if we can find out anything in the region of Chauncy Street in the East End, which appears to be where all this business really began some twenty-five years ago.'

'Our only hope, sir,' Grimshaw admitted; then with a troubled look he added: 'With Claire Wilton out of the picture, and the woman who called at the Jackson's probably being a normal business caller, we — '

'A moment,' Hancock interrupted hurriedly, swallowing the remains of a sandwich. 'In regard to that, an idea occurs to me. I don't know why I didn't think of it before.'

He reached to the telephone and raised it, giving instructions to be put through to the Jackson residence. It was the voice of Ella that presently responded.

'Inspector Hancock here, Ella,' the Chief Inspector said. 'Mr. Jackson at home?'

'Yes, sir, he just got in. Hang on a minute . . . '

There was a pause and the sound of somebody approaching the instrument, then George Jackson's somber lifeless tones came through. It was more than obvious that the grim demise of his wife was weighing heavily upon him.

'Hello, Inspector. Something I can do for you?'

'I think there is, Mr. Jackson, yes — and it may help very materially. Has Ella told you about a woman who called on the day your wife . . . met her death?'

'Yes, she has. As a matter of fact I've been trying to think who it could have been. She must know from the papers that I'm back in town, but she hasn't communicated again.'

'You mean you haven't any idea as to her identity?'

'Not the slightest. I've been enquiring of my various staffs in the chain stores I run, but apparently none of them seem able to account for the visit. In any case, I don't conduct business from my home. It's all done from head office. I understand she was tall, dark and slim, and wearing thick spectacles. It's all quite beyond me.'

'That woman, Mr. Jackson, was the killer,' Hancock said quietly. 'I'm convinced of it now. She rang first to see how the land lay at your home — and learned you and your wife had gone to your beach cottage. She managed to cajole the address out of Ella — and she being a youngster, didn't hesitate much over giving it. Look — put Ella on the phone again. I want to see if she can remember any other details about her.'

'Right — ' There was the sound of George Jackson's voice at a distance. 'Ella — come here a moment. The inspector wants a word with you.'

Ella's voice came through a trifle nervously. 'Yes, sir.'

'Ella,' Hancock said, 'in describing that woman visitor to me you said she was about thirty, fairly tall and slim, with dark hair and wearing thick glasses. That's a pretty general description, and typical of millions of women . . . Can you think of any specific peculiarity about her? Some little thing in her bearing, voice, or manner — or even in the form of jewelry or ear-rings, which might distinguish her?'

'I'll — have to think,' Ella muttered.

'By all means do . . . I can wait.' Hancock sat back in his chair and sipped tea from his cup at intervals. Sergeant Grimshaw munched a sandwich and waited with interest — then he saw his superior become intent again as the voice came back in the receiver. Grimshaw could not tell what was being said — to his irritation — but he saw a gleam of triumph come into Hancock's pale eyes.

'It was, eh?' he said at last. 'Thank you, Ella! I do believe you've put us on the right track at last. Bye.'

He put the phone down and grinned widely. The sergeant raised an eyebrow.

'Looks like you've got something, sir,' he commented.

'You bet I have, Harry — but I've got to verify everything before I dare believe it. Incredible though it may seem that girl Ella remembered something about the killer which positively identifies her — but the why and wherefore has yet to be checked.'

'There's only one woman in this business,' Grimshaw pointed out. 'Claire

Wilton — and she's as good as been proven innocent.'

'If you look through the notes, you'll find two other women — one is Mary Hilliard, Derek Cantrill's potential fiancée — and who, according to the man I have watching Cantrill, threw Cantrill overboard for some reason or other; and the other woman is the third, as yet unfound, sister.'

'Who, if she's like her other two sisters, should be blonde and not dark.'

'There are such things as wigs and hair-dye. Or if you don't like the sound of that, Mary Hilliard is dark anyway, and fairly tall.'

Grimshaw rubbed his chin pensively, then his gaze strayed back to the Chief Inspector's twinkling eyes.

'Forgive me saying it, sir, but I have the idea you're just kidding.'

Hancock grinned widely. 'Maybe I am. Anyway it's safer than saying something outright before I've proved it.'

★   ★   ★

The following morning, about the time Hancock and Grimshaw set off to investigate the East End, Janice Mottram was making final arrangements for her departure for France, her actual leave-taking being timed for noon, the boat train leaving Victoria at 12-20. The morning papers which concerned themselves with social news carried due information concerning the fact. Whether or not the killer would be aware of it, Janice did not know. In her heart she was quite convinced that sooner or later the killer would catch up with her — and she was prepared in full for that moment when it came.

Barrington and Mrs. Bates were already briefed as to what they would have to do. It would be their duty to follow Janice on the 8-0 p.m. train, by which time she herself would be nearing her destination. What she did not know was that her husband, acting on his own initiative — and for the sole reason that he was afraid for her safety — was trying frantically to get in touch with Hancock. He, not being sure of his

186

movements, could not be located despite sundry efforts by squad cars to get in touch with him. Actually, he and Grimshaw were far from their police car when their short-wave radio came to life to summon them. So, in the end, Richard Mottram had to give it up, stolidly refusing to entrust his information to any other officer. Finally he came round to thinking that perhaps it was in the right order of things that he had been unable to contact the Chief Inspector. He had promised Janice to keep quiet — and circumstances were enforcing him to keep his word.

The killer, for her part, never saw the announcement in the society columns concerning Janice's intended vacation. Indeed she had no need to bother looking; her attention was concentrated on the Mottram home itself. She watched it quite openly, and those who passed by her had not the vaguest idea of what was intended. Crescent Avenue, wherein the Mottram residence stood, was tree-lined, with a wooden seat every two dozen yards or so. Upon one of these the murderess was seated, enjoying the sunlight, her eyes constantly watching the Mottram home. Further away up the Crescent, almost where it joined the main road, was an old but reliable M.G. Midget, the killer's property — nobody aware that she possessed it save she herself.

Thus it was that when she left her home at noon, deep in the cushions of the Rolls, Janice had no idea that the killer was quickly on her tail. In an idle glance through the limousine's rear window she saw the M. G. Midget plainly enough some distance away, once the main road was reached — but thought nothing of it. Once amidst the full swirl of the city-bound traffic the fast little car was lost to sight — but to the eyes of the killer the Rolls was not so easily escapable. Its smooth lines stood out a mile, and it was relentlessly pursued as far as Victoria station.

Here the killer only just had time to park her M.G. on the public ground adjoining the station, then she hurried to mix with the throngs heading for the platforms. At first she was chagrined as she thought she had lost sight of Janice altogether; then for just an instant she caught a glimpse of her saucy hat near No. 8 booking office. That was enough. Janice walked on to the platform of the south-bound boat train — Barrington having arranged her luggage for her in advance and then departing — entirely unaware that not three yards behind her was the woman who was intent on destroying her. Knowing perfectly well that she would not be recognized without a good deal of careful scrutiny on Janice's part, the murderess was at no particular pains to hide herself.

Janice entered the train and went along the corridor until she arrived at an empty first-class compartment. She entered it, selected a corner seat, and settled down to read. She hoped that she would have the compartment to herself, but as the train got on the move, the hope was shattered. The woman who had followed her came into the compartment, shut the door, and settled in the corner diagonally across from Janice. Janice raised her eyes for a moment to look at the newcomer, then lowered them again to her magazine. With a steady clock of wheels over rail joints the local express began to gather speed.

The murderess sat apparently half dozing in her corner until the ticket collector had been his rounds; then with the train doing a good fifty miles an hour at the peak of its trip to the south coast, the woman rose and crossed to the corner directly opposite Janice. Janice looked up in some surprise and drew in her slightly outstretched feet.

'Look at me carefully, Janice,' the murderess said, smiling. 'I do believe you don't recognize me.'

Janice looked, frozenly, so utterly taken off her guard her mind would not function for the moment. With all the plans she had laid, the last thing she had expected was that the killer would turn up on the train itself.

'Would you like me to refresh your memory?' the woman asked, her smile fading and her eyes becoming bright and hard. 'Go back down the years — to childhood and the early teens . . . '

Janice stared, then as a bend in the line caused the sunlight to fall directly upon the killer's face, Janice gave a little gasp.

'You!' she breathed in amazement. 'Grown up — !'

'Most people grow up,' the woman replied cynically. 'You seem to have done it in luxury, too, like your precious sisters.'

She got to her feet suddenly and went over to the corridor side of the compartment. Swiftly she drew down the blinds and dropped the catch on the door. She turned just in time to see Janice groping for the automatic in her bag. Before she could get it out the woman had seized the bag in her strong fingers, lowered the window on to the up-line, and thrown the bag and its contents to the winds.

'You won't need that,' she said, sitting down again and smiling bitterly.

Janice remained motionless, her eyes round in horror. Of the three sisters, she had always been the most nervous. The knowledge that she was locked in with the killer bereft her of the power to think or move. The wind from the open window stirred the fair hair that had tumbled loosely about her forehead from under her saucy hat.

'I think you should know,' the woman said moodily, 'that I did not really want to kill either Vera or Elsie. It was just that I had to do it because otherwise I could have been nailed by the police — and the stakes are too high to permit of that.'

Janice forced herself to speak even though her throat felt cracked.

'You wanted to know what was written on their backs, didn't you?'

'Of course. Just as I mean to know what's written on yours. You see, I've been in the unfortunate position that I haven't got things in the right order. Had I got Vera and then you, instead of Vera and then Elsie, I could have been saved a lot of trouble. The name split in three would have made sense with one end and the middle — but with just the two ends and no middle, it failed to click. Understand?'

'I — I can't think why you needed to go to these lengths. Surely you could have remembered the tattoos. You saw them often enough in the past.'

'As a youngster, yes — but youngsters have notoriously short memories. I couldn't for the life of me recall the tattooed letters, when latterly I realized their significance. Vera's really to blame for all this trouble, you know. If she had changed her name, as you two others did, I'd never have been able to do anything. As it was I had only to trace her and she told me all I wanted to know.'

The train rattled and quivered as it swung over the points and thereafter raced onwards at fifty miles an hour. Janice cleared her throat.

'I can tell you what the tattoo is on my back if you want. It's 'Lil.' L-I-L.'

'Mary — Ian — Lil,' the woman said. 'Doesn't make sense — but wait!' Her eyes gleamed. 'Yes, it does! Mary — Lil — Ian — Mary Lilian!'

'Yes,' Janice whispered, staring at her. 'Mary Lilian. That's it . . . '

'Good. Thanks for telling me — and thanks too for being obliging. But I'm afraid it won't do you any good. For one thing I must check it for myself, and for another I can never allow you to have the chance of saying what has gone on in this carriage.'

Janice remained silent. The murderess sat thinking for a moment, puzzling something out to herself. Janice's eyes strayed from her at last and to the countryside flying past outside. Her gaze moved on and up to the communication cord. Suddenly, in one tremendous dive, she jumped up and tried to grasp it. Just as her fingers struck it a blow under the jaw knocked her reeling, to crash on the floor at the other side of the compartment.

'You would, would you?' the woman asked softly. 'Not if I know it, Janice! And you're not going to get the chance to cry out, either.'

Janice made a sudden effort to get up from the floor, but the hands of the woman came down towards her, gripped her throat, crushed tighter and ever tighter with terrifying power.

Five minutes later the express roared on its way into a tunnel. When it emerged

194

again the murderess was seated by herself in a corner seat. She gave a start as a train on the up-line suddenly slammed and rattled past in a confusion of steam. Then as a thought seemed to strike her she smiled.

9

It was mid-afternoon before Chief Inspector Hancock and Sergeant Grimshaw picked up anything interesting in the way of information, and this came from a confectioner who ran a fly-blown shop at the railway-siding end of Chauncy Street, where, from all accounts, Arthur Bradmore had once lived with his wife and triplets.

The confectioner, a middle-aged, mournful-looking individual, registered no particular emotion when Hancock exhibited his warrant-card. Police were not uncommon visitors in this low-class neighborhood, so one more did not make much difference.

'Lived here long?' Hancock asked pleasantly, half leaning on the counter and passing a dubious eye over dusty cakes and biscuit tins.

'Thirty-five years,' the man answered, suspicion in his murky gray eyes. 'Can't see what difference it makes to a busy like you. I runs my business legitimate.'

'You can run it how you like for all I care,' Hancock assured him, straightening up and lighting his pipe. 'I just want to find out if your memory will work over twenty or thirty years . . . Ever hear of Arthur Bradmore, a tattooist?'

'Yes, 'course I did. That girl who was smothered recently — Vera Bradmore — was his daughter. One of 'em, anyway. I knew her pitcher the moment it was in the paper. When I read about that tattoo on her back I was dead sure.'

'I can see you're going to be a great help,' Hancock decided. 'How about fixing up some tea and — er — cakes for two hungry policemen, while we talk?'

'Well, I . . . Okay,' the man agreed, and went into the back regions to investigate possibilities. After an interminable time he returned with two cups of steaming tea, a tumbler filled with sugar, and a motion towards the cakes.

''Elp yourself, gents. Tea's threepence a cup an' each cake is tuppence.'

'Mmmm — dirt cheap,' Hancock

grinned; but the proprietor seemed to miss the point.

'I suppose,' he said, resting his bony elbows on the counter and peering at Hancock confidentially, 'I might figure sort of prominent in this case if I can help you?'

Hancock drank some tea. 'Maybe. You should have come forward and told us something without being asked, of course — so don't expect to turn into too much of a glamour boy. Anyway, to get down to business. I take it you knew about that tattoo on Vera Bradmore's back?'

''Course I did. So did everybody around here — at that time. I'm the only one left now. Must be twenty years ago since the Bradmores was here.'

'Uh-huh. There were three girls, were there not? Triplets?'

'Aye. Never could tell 'em apart. Each of 'em with a tattoo on their back.'

'How can you be so sure of that?' Sergeant Grimshaw put in. 'We know that the tattoo was low down in the case of Vera Bradmore — and also in the case of Elsie Jackson — '

'Elsie Jackson was another of the sisters,' the proprietor put in. 'Not that I seen her photo in the paper, but what I read about a tattoo, an' her being like Vera, decided me. So I said to myself — '

'Never mind what you said to yourself,' Hancock intervened. 'How did you know about these tattoos? The kids didn't run about naked, did they?'

'Nearly,' the proprietor grinned. 'You know what it is with kids in a neighborhood like this — but that wasn't how I knew. My sister, you see, used t'do a bit of charring an' cleaning in those days — she's dead now — an' one of the women she helped was Milly Whittaker. Milly Whittaker was a friend of Mrs. Bradmore, just as Jim Whittaker was a close friend of Arthur Bradmore. So, when Arthur sent his kids into the care of Mr. and Mrs. Whittaker — which they did after he got himself killed — my sister often saw the triplets being bathed and put to bed while she cleaned up the house.'

Hancock passed a hand over his eyes uncertainly and took another gulp of tea.

'Not exactly lucid, are you?' he asked, sighing. 'I've got to get this lot cleared up properly. Now, let's start again. Arthur Bradmore got himself killed, you say. How?'

The proprietor hesitated, so the Chief Inspector added, 'On June 4th, 1924 — twenty-five years ago — Arthur Bradmore was killed while resisting arrest for a diamond robbery. That much we do know, so don't start wrapping anything up.'

'Yes, that's right,' the proprietor admitted. 'It was when the police were closing in that Bradmore sent his kids over to Jim and Milly Whittaker — the only friends he could trust — then he and his wife tried to make a break for it and were killed in a roof-top hunt. The police were around here for days after, making enquiries and getting nowhere. Those diamonds were never found, y'know.'

'I'm well aware of it . . . ' Hancock tried one of the cakes and found it better than it looked. 'So, before being arrested — and being killed trying to evade it, along with his wife — he sent the three children to Jim and Milly Whittaker. Okay — and where did they live?'

''Bout two miles from here, in Vildon Street. Near the brewery.'

'Mmmm — very salubrious. Then, as I see it, your sister — in helping Mrs. Whittaker — noticed these tattoos on the children's backs. Did she ever say what the tattoos said?'

'She did, yes — but I don't remember them. Anyway, you know from the two bodies that have been found, don't you? One said 'Mary' and the other 'Ian.' I've no idea what the third one said. I wasn't interested . . . matter of fact I didn't like the notion a bit. I said to myself, a man who'll tattoo his own kids like that must be a snake. It hurts does tattooing. Look, I've got a dancin' girl on my chest, an' it hurt plenty to have it put there. The needle stings — '

'I'm not interested in your chest,' Hancock said sourly. 'But I agree the needle hurts. Must have given those youngsters quite a bit of torture. Which,' he said, 'is a bit odd. Bradmore loved his children enough to make a desperate effort to send them to safety; yet he tattooed each one. Mmmm . . . '

The only sound for a moment was Grimshaw stirring his tea. Then Hancock asked a further question.

'After these three children had been handed over to Mr. and Mrs. Whittaker, what happened? Any idea? Did they legally adopt them?'

'I dunno exactly — but I do know that they went on living with the Whittakers . . . ' The proprietor reflected. 'Aye, they must have been nearly sixteen or thereabouts before the parting came.'

'Parting?' Hancock looked up over his teacup.

'It was this way, y'see,' the proprietor continued, thoroughly enjoying himself as the sole possessor of the information. 'The Whittakers had a kid of their own — a girl about a year older than the three triplets. What in heck was her name now . . . ? Oh, I remember! Sybil! That was it. Used to seem sort of a swanky name. Kids made fun of it around here.'

'I can imagine,' Hancock agreed, cuffing his trilby up on to his forehead and noting that Grimshaw was writing down all the information. 'So there were triplets and one girl a year older — Sybil Whittaker. Now what about this parting of the ways business? How'd you mean?'

'When they got to sixteen the three kids just left the neighborhood,' the proprietor said. 'No idea where they went. They was nearly young women, of course. I'd seen 'em grow up. I suppose they got jobs. But Whittaker, his missus, and Sybil emigrated to South Africa under some sort of Government scheme. I never heard of 'em after that.'

There was silence. Grimshaw's eyes met those of his superior. The Chief Inspector put some money on the counter to pay for the teas and cakes.

'And that's all you can tell us?' he asked.

''Fraid it is, sir . . . ' The cash register clanged. 'Your change, sir — thank you.'

'Look,' Hancock said, straightening his hat, 'does the tattoo business suggest anything to you? The names of 'Mary' and 'Ian' for instance?'

'Can't say it does.'

'Have you any idea what Jim Whittaker did for a living?'

'Well, he said he was a plumber by trade — but I heard lots of rumors.'

'Rumors carry truth sometimes. What were they?'

'Far as I could make out he and Arthur Bradmore were mixed up in a lot of petty crime — thieving on a small scale, and such. That big diamond robbery Bradmore got mixed up in may have included Whittaker too. I don't now. But I do know the busies never picked him for it — so either he had nothing to do with it, or they couldn't pin anything on him.'

Hancock meditated for a moment or two, then he gave his genial grin.

'Well, all things being equal, that seems to be about all we can find out here. Thanks very much — and, by the way, take that aspidistra out of the window. They like a shady, cool place. Come on, Harry.'

The sergeant nodded and followed his superior outside. As they strolled along the dreary, squalid street in the warm afternoon sunlight, it was plain Hancock was doing a good deal of thinking.

'Having a pretty good idea who the killer is — unless I'm working on an unforgivable coincidence — isn't such a help as I thought it would be,' he commented presently, tugging out his pipe and banging it on the brickwork of the building he was passing. 'It's the devil's own job to find the right proof for everything. What we have learned from our friend with the anaemic cakes is helpful, of course — though in another sense it confuses the issue.'

'I may as well be frank, sir, and confess that I've lost track of everything completely,' Grimshaw sighed. 'I can plainly see that Bradmore, the tattooist, handed his kids over to Jim Whittaker before he and his wife were killed . . . but what in blazes did he tattoo names on their backs for? It just doesn't make sense!'

'It has to — or he wouldn't have done.' Hancock refilled his pipe as he walked; then lighted it. 'Yes, Harry, it has to — but I seem to be inconceivably dunderheaded in not being able to see the point.'

'Apparently Jim Whittaker never saw the point either because, far as we can tell, nothing ever came of those tattoos. The triplets lived with the Whittakers until they became young women — then presumably they went off into the big, cold world of their own accord, and the Whittakers went to South Africa. All like a nice, family story in a Sunday magazine.'

'I think the best thing we can do is take a look at the newspapers for round about June 4th, 1924, and see what we can find out from them. There might be some clue in the descriptions of that diamond robbery.'

'Good idea, sir,' Grimshaw agreed — and having again a focal point for their activities, they increased pace and gained their parked car a few minutes later.

Grimshaw drove direct to Fleet Street and before long he and Hancock were both studying the newspaper files for May, June, and July, 1924, in an ante-room of one of London's most famous evening paper's offices.

It was Grimshaw who first alighted

upon something, in the issue for June 2nd, 1924. He drew Hancock's attention to it quickly and together they read:

'This afternoon there was an armed hold-up at the premises of Messrs. Dagnall & Farson, the well-known jewelers in Upper Bond Street. Two men, leaving a car with its engine running, entered the shop and, at the point of a gun, emptied the showcases of trays of diamonds to the approximate value of £100,000, quite the biggest haul ever made by thieves. They attempted no violence. As they left, however, two passers-by realized what had happened and gave the alarm. The two thieves had no time to reach their car. They parted company, and escaped — the man who had taken the diamonds, which were in an attaché case, heading east. He was lost in the crowd before he could be caught; his accomplice also got away.

'Questioned later by the police, the staff of the jewelry store stated that the man with the gun had been masked with a handkerchief and was not easily identifiable. He was tallish and broad shouldered. The other man, who took the diamonds, was masked to begin with, but in reaching over a showcase, the end of the handkerchief caught between his body and the showcase edge, which revealed his features before he could cover them again. He is described as about 35-37, medium height, dark-haired. Investigation is now proceeding.'

'In other words,' Hancock said, 'our friend Arthur Bradmore was the one with the dislodged face-mask. What else is there?'

He began searching later issues, but the next worthwhile announcement concerned the actual closing-in of the police upon Bradmore's home in Chauncy Street. The report ran:

'This afternoon, Arthur Bradmore, wanted by the police in connection with the recent £100,000 diamond robbery in Upper Bond Street, was killed in a thrilling roof-top struggle as he tried to escape. His wife, who was with him, was also killed when they made a death leap. This, it is believed by the police, was not intentional, but occurred through them failing to clear the space between two buildings and falling seventy feet to a concrete alley instead.

'The diamonds, which were in Bradmore's possession when stolen, have not been found — and he died without revealing their hiding place. The three children of Arthur Bradmore — triplets, whom he sent for safety to a friend as he tried to make his getaway — have been seen by the police, but are too young to be of service.

'Police investigation to trace the partner of Bradmore and recover the diamonds will continue.'

'And evidently has petered out,' Hancock said. 'From the C.R.O. records we know that the diamonds were never found . . . Mmmm. This, Harry, takes thinking about . . . '

Just as if he were in his own office at Whitehall, he sat back at the broad filing desk and lighted his pipe.

'I believe I begin to see the first dim signs of daylight,' he muttered. 'It's strange that Bradmore, on the run, and knowing his features had been seen by the jewelry store staff, took such a risk as to come to his own home, where he must have known the police would catch up with him quicker than any other way. I say it's strange unless he had a mighty good reason.'

'What reason, sir?'

'Look at it this way. Let us assume — and safely too, I think — that Jim Whittaker was the accomplice, the man who had the gun and whose mask prevented him being identified . . . '

'Possible,' Grimshaw agreed, after due thought. 'Only the police would surely have suspected him when they went round to see the three triplets? Surely they would have probed him in every possible way knowing he was an intimate friend of Bradmore's — as obviously he was by being trusted enough to take care of the three children.'

'They could have probed him until Doomsday, Harry — but, as you know, without proof, they couldn't do a thing. Where was that proof? His features were not seen by anybody during the robbery. We can be sure he disposed of his gun

— and he had no diamonds because Bradmore took charge of them. The police could not do a thing. They'd be nailed by that irritating clause — 'benefit of the doubt,' which is such a bugbear to us police. So,' Hancock said, 'assume he was accomplice. Let us also assume that Bradmore knew he was sunk and being watched, yet wanted to pass on to his friend the whereabouts of the jewels he had hidden. How could he do it? By letter, wire, or telephone — even personal messenger — he would be taped. If he sent the kids to blurt it out to Whittaker, the police might overhear. So — what then?'

Grimshaw gave a little start. 'I get it. He tattooed the information on the backs of the three children; and then sent them to Whittaker under the very noses of the police. That way he would rid himself of the burden of three young children when he wanted to try and escape, and also — he hoped — Whittaker would know what he meant and find the diamonds.'

'That, as I see it, is the answer,' Hancock muttered, peering into vacancy.

'But something must have gone wrong because, according to our friend with the dusty cakes, Whittaker lived on in that sordid district for roughly another thirteen years. A man who had access to a hundred thousand in gems wouldn't do that. There are two answers: he either decided to go straight and let the past die with Bradmore; or else he couldn't make head or tail of the tattoos when he saw them. I assume he must have seen them at some time or other but possibly they made no more sense to him than they do to us.'

'They make sense to one person, anyway,' Grimshaw said grimly. 'The present killer!'

'Yes . . . how very true. The killer is a woman, of that I am sure, and if a certain long-shot assumption of mine is correct I know which woman — but it has to be tied up with Sybil Whittaker, the daughter of Jim and Milly Whittaker. At seventeen, approximately — since she was a year older than the triplets — she and her parents went to South Africa. After which . . . what happened?'

'You mean,' Grimshaw said slowly, 'that the killer might be Sybil Whittaker?'

'Why not? She might have been keener mentally than her father and interpreted from the tattoos — which she must often have seen — what they meant. That could only have come about if at some time her father had let something slip concerning the robbery. It is possible that Sybil has a mind like her father's — unscrupulous, maybe. Tempt a woman with the certain knowledge that she can find a hundred thousand pounds in diamonds, and give her a ruthless nature, and nothing will stop her. That may have happened here, but it's mainly assumption. Our next move is to contact the emigration officials in South Africa and find out what they can give us on the Whittaker family. With the help of the South African police, we can probably piece together the final links in this complicated chain.'

'And yet you know who the killer is right this moment?' Grimshaw asked. 'Why not make an arrest and get the story afterwards?'

'Because, Harry, when I make an arrest

I have to make it stick, backed by irrefutable facts. Until then I've got to lie low. Legal technicality — blast it — demands it. Also, there is the chance I may have guessed wrong, for I am working on what could be coincidence, and if so I don't want to put my foot in it.' Hancock glanced up at the clock. 'We'd better be on our way,' he said, rising. 'See if anything's turned up at the office.'

He turned towards the door and then paused as a reporter whom he knew well came in.

'Oh, hello, Inspector. They told me you were in here.'

'Large as life,' Hancock said, smiling. 'How did that grass seed I recommended go on?'

'Oh, fine — fine.' The reporter seemed anxious to dismiss the topic. 'Look, inspector, I think I've got some news for you,' he hurried on. 'From what you've been telling the papers, you have been anxious to find a third sister resembling Vera Bradmore and Elsie Jackson, haven't you?'

'You bet I have!' Eagerness kindled in Hancock's pale eyes. 'Why, have you found her?'

'I haven't, no, but I'm covering the story. The news editor has just tipped me off to get down to Carter's Fold — '

'Where the devil's that?'

'About half way between London and the south coast. A woman's body has been found on the railway line, horribly mangled from all accounts. She's identical to the two women who have been recently murdered.'

'With — with a tattoo on her back?' Hancock asked, looking dazed.

'There are traces of one, but she's so cut up the tattoo mark has been obliterated, according to what news I've had on the telephone from the police down there.'

'Damn!' Hancock breathed savagely. 'Oh — damn! The very last link, and it can't be read — !'

'Her name's Janice Mottram, wife of Richard Mottram, the big perfumier. Her bag was found some seven miles from her body with particulars in it. In other words, Inspector, it looks as though that third sister has been found — too late.'

'Thanks, anyway,' Hancock said curtly. 'Let's get back to the Yard, Harry. We've no time to waste . . . '

★　★　★

When he arrived back at his office, Hancock found that quite a few things had been happening in his absence. He was promptly informed as to the efforts that had been made to get in touch with him — at the behest of Richard Mottram — and there were also reports still coming in concerning the woman's body found on the railway line.

Grimmer than Sergeant Grimshaw had yet seen him, Hancock brooded over the information in the form of reports before him.

'This is bad, Harry — damned bad,' he said at last, a bleak look in his pale eyes. 'Through sheer chance we didn't happen to be handy when Janice's husband rang through — and because of it this has happened. Not that I know even now what he wanted, but I'll wager it might have prevented Janice's death.'

He scowled at the report in his hands.

'Severely injured,' he muttered. 'Signs of manual strangulation about the throat. Tattoo mark on small of back obliterated by injuries. Only one answer to that one. The killer was on the train, strangled Janice, and then threw her out of the window. Which means the killer now has all three names and, presumably, the matter is complete as far as she is concerned.'

'Doesn't seem the police down there have got very far in tracing the killer, either,' Grimshaw commented, reading more reports. 'They've checked at Victoria and all stations touched by the train and haven't found a thing.'

'And I don't expect they will, either,' Hancock frowned. 'The killer would walk off the train in the usual way, I expect, and who on earth would know she was the killer? In just the same way how could anybody know anything about her as she got on the train? She's worked as simply — and yet as craftily

— as on all other occasions.'

There was silence; then Grimshaw asked:

'What moves are you going to make then, sir?'

'As far as Janice is concerned, none at all. I'll leave it to the police down there to investigate. She can't be of use to us with the tattoo obliterated, and I've too many other angles to examine — which should lead to the killer — to go dashing off at a tangent. What I do want to know, though, is what Richard Mottram could have wanted — '

Hancock broke off and aimed an eye towards the door as a constable came in.

'A Mr. Mottram to see you, sir,' he announced.

'Talk of the devil,' Hancock muttered, getting to his feet; then in a few seconds he was shaking hands with the pink-faced, placid-eyed perfumier as he came into the office.

'Have a seat, Mr. Mottram.' Hancock motioned. 'I'm glad that at last you've managed to get hold of me. I believe you've been trying most of the day to talk to me.'

'And because I couldn't, my wife has been murdered,' Mottram stated, his voice coldly malicious. 'To my way of thinking that makes you almost directly responsible for her death.'

'I am glad you qualified your remark with 'almost',' Hancock answered quietly. 'While I can well understand your distress, sir, I cannot hold myself responsible for what has happened. I've been busy with investigation all day; it is not always possible to keep in touch with headquarters.'

Mottram was silent, his hands working with his lemon-colored gloves as they lay on the desk.

'I'm sorry,' he apologized finally, with a distraught glance. 'The news of Janice's brutal death has been such a shock to me I — I hardly realize what I'm saying or doing.'

Hancock was silent. He returned to his swivel chair and waited. Grimshaw moved to his desk and prepared his notebook.

'When my wife was found, the police got in touch with me,' he explained. 'They obtained all the particulars from the contents of her handbag. You see, I knew this might happen, which was why I tried to find you.'

'You should have given your information to somebody,' Hancock said. 'It would have been realized it was a matter of life and death and I would have been reached somehow. Without any apparent real need of urgency, no particular effort was made.'

'I realize now that I should have done more,' Mottram said unhappily.

'You say you knew this might happen,' Hancock remarked. 'How do you mean?'

Richard Mottram did not waste any more time telling the story of Janice's intentions. When he had finished, the Chief Inspector gave a sigh.

'A commendable effort on her part, Mr. Mottram, but a deadly one,' he said bitterly. 'It cost her . . . her life. However, there is one interesting fact in it all that may be invaluable to us. You knew your wife had a tattoo on her back, you say?'

'Yes, indeed. I found it out accidentally last summer. Her swimsuit caught on a rock and ripped; that was when the tattoo was revealed. I would have liked to question it, but Janice and I had an understanding that we trusted each other — no matter what.'

'What did the tattoo say?'

'It was a woman's name — 'Lil.' Had it been the name of a man I would probably have felt jealous. As it was I was puzzled, but nothing more.'

Hancock wrote 'L-I-L' on his scratch-pad and then said:

'Your wife, apparently, was afraid to explain anything to you for fear of social repercussions. That is understandable, Mr. Mottram. I can tell you exactly what she was afraid of. You had better know, because when the newspapers come out with all the details — as they will when this case is brought to a conclusion — you might get a decided shock. Your wife, and Vera Bradmore and Elsie Jackson, were the triplet daughters of a robber, a hold-up man.'

'The daughters of — a criminal, do you mean?' Mottram stared aghast.

'I'm afraid so. Now you can understand why your wife did not wish to reveal anything. It would have meant admitting that her father stole a hundred thousand pounds' worth of diamonds twenty-five odd years ago, and was killed — with his wife — while attempting to escape from the police.'

Richard Mottram was silent for a long time. Then with an effort, he seemed to pull himself together.

'Thank you for telling me, Inspector. Whatever Janice's upbringing may have been, she was the sweetest woman in the world in my eyes — and I'll never rest until her murderer is brought to justice. Whatever I can do, in any possible way, I will do.'

'That's nice to know, sir.' Hancock got to his feet again and came round the desk. 'I don't wish to seem brusque amidst your distress, Mr. Mottram, but you can help me best by doing nothing at all.'

'Oh?'

'I mean that I have matters so arranged now that I think I can spring a trap. In regard to your wife, you will attend the inquest — which, as in the case of the previous two inquests — will be adjourned until our enquiries are complete; then you will please attend to your own business and leave me to attend to mine. At this stage there is nothing else you can usefully do.'

Mottram nodded and got to his feet, taking up his hat and gloves.

'I understand, Inspector — and please forgive my earlier remark when I came in here.'

'Of course.' With a serious smile Hancock saw him out of the office. Sergeant Grimshaw rose from his desk, his usually impassive face excited.

' 'Lil,' sir!' he exclaimed. 'Now we've got all three names! Mary — Ian — Lil.'

'Uh-huh . . . ' Hancock returned to his swivel chair and dragged out his pipe. He lit it as he pondered. Finally, he said: 'Get me South Africa House, Harry — emigration department.'

Disappointed at his superior's apparent lack of interest in the three mystery names — but taking care not to show it — Grimshaw did as he was ordered; then he handed the phone over.

'C.I.D. here,' Hancock said. 'Inspector Hancock speaking . . . I want some information. Can you trace the emigration of a family of three, by the names of Mr. and Mrs. James Whittaker, and daughter Sybil, aged seventeen, in the year 1937? I don't know which month. It was a Government-assisted scheme, or something.' He waited and then said, 'Okay, thanks!' and put the phone back on its cradle.

'They'll ring me back,' he said, seeing Grimshaw's look of enquiry. 'Take a cable, Harry — no, never mind,' he corrected himself. 'Better see where they landed in South Africa before I do that . . . Now, let's see.'

He swung round in his swivel chair so that he faced the huge and somewhat dusty map of London on the wall. Grimshaw was left staring at the back of his superior's close-cropped head. He fully believed that Hancock was considering the evening sky through the grimy window and weighing up weather prospects for his garden — but in another moment he knew differently.

'It isn't 'Mary — Ian — Lil,' Harry,' he said. 'That would be crazy. It's 'Mary — Lil — Ian'.'

'Oh,' Grimshaw said, nonplussed. 'Frankly, sir, it sounds about the same either way.'

'It does? Then try this — There's a big station in this city by the name of Marybonele. That make sense?'

'You mean Marylebone, don't you? Oh — wait!' The sergeant gave a start. 'Mary Lilian!' he said. 'Mary Lilian Station! But there isn't one,' he finished, musing.

'But there is Mary Lilian *Street*,' Hancock said. 'I'm looking at it right now — clearly marked. See . . . ' He rose to his feet and jabbed his pipe-stem on the map. Grimshaw came over to look and found Mary Lilian Street plainly revealed.

'Pretty near the docks and Chauncy Street,' he said.

'That's right, sir! How on earth did you ever guess that?'

'I didn't exactly guess it; it fitted automatically when I knew the last name was 'Lil.' We've satisfied ourselves the names don't refer to people; the only other thing could be a street. Since we're looking for somewhere where Bradmore might have hidden the diamonds the answer came naturally — in Mary Lilian Street, not so very far from his home.'

'And yet Whittaker apparently never tumbled to it!'

'No — perhaps because his home in Vildon Street is much further away, and Mary Lilian Street was possibly unknown to him.'

'Yes, sir, that's it,' Grimshaw breathed, after a thoughtful silence. 'See — Mary Lilian Street is not so far away from where Chauncy Street is, and it's also situated due south — from which direction Bradmore must have come in his escape from Upper Bond Street . . . down here.'

'Right,' Hancock agreed. Then after a moment he added, 'This map is a 1936 one; never been replaced. 'Bout time it was, considering the blitz that's been since. I have an idea that — '

He swung to the telephone and picked it up, silencing its ringing.

'Yes? Inspector Hancock speaking . . . Oh, yes, South Africa House — Uh-huh.

Yes — Whittaker. That's it. James, Milly or Mildred, and daughter Sybil — They did? Good! Cape Town, eh? Yes, that's all thanks. I should be able to get the rest from the authorities in Cape Town. Much obliged. Bye.'

He put the phone down again and glanced at Grimshaw. 'I don't need to explain that, Harry; you gathered it. They went to Cape Town. Take a cable, will you — to the Chief of Police, Cape Town, South Africa . . . Er — 'Require all details concerning James, Mildred, and Sybil Whittaker, who arrived in Capetown somewhere in August, 1937. State if still alive or where they can be reached. Very urgent. Cable reply. Hancock C.I.D.' That should about cover it. Whilst you fix it up I'm taking a trip to Mary Lilian Street.'

'You won't need me there then, sir?' Grimshaw asked, disappointed.

'Not this time, Harry. I'm only going to look, so don't feel too badly about it. Stay until I get back. If we leave this office empty again and something serious happens we'll never hear the last of it!'

10

When Hancock returned to the office it was nearly half-past nine. Grimshaw was lounging at his desk, the typing of all his notes complete. He was in the middle of stifling a yawn as his superior came in.

'If you're tired of waiting, I don't blame you,' Hancock said dryly. He cuffed up his hat and went over to the intercom, on his desk, pressing down a switch. 'Detail six men to watch Mary Lilian Street, East Central, from cover,' he said. 'Arrange for reliefs. That street is to be watched day and night and the moment a woman is seen searching there pick her up and bring her in. Got that — ? Okay.'

He switched off again and rubbed his hands gently together.

'Which, my boy,' he said genially, 'wraps the whole business up in a bag. It's finished. Complete. All I've got to do now is watch the killer walk into the trap — as she surely will do after all the trouble she's been to. Then she will stand self-convicted and that, with the evidence I've accrued against her, will be sufficient. Come to think of it, I could pick her up this very moment if my guess is right, but — ' He shook his head. 'No; we'll see if she bites now she's got the names from all three backs.'

'You had a look at Mary Lilian Street then, sir?' Grimshaw asked, still somewhat aggrieved.

'I did indeed. Grand night too!' Hancock wagged his bullet head. 'Bring on those young sweet peas of mine in great style. Mild and gentle, with a touch of rain in the wind.'

Grimshaw nodded gloomily and said nothing more. The sweet peas could go to blazes for all he cared; it was Mary Lilian Street he wanted to know about. It occurred to him he might have a look at it before he went home; then he changed his mind. With police assigned to watch it he'd have to explain his presence, and that in turn would make Hancock want to know why —

'I think we can wrap it up for tonight,

Harry,' Hancock said, glancing at the clock. 'Nothing more we can do and we've got to sleep, same as anybody else. If anything happens I'll know about it soon enough in the morning.'

He turned and led the way to the door. Grimshaw took down his hat and coat from the peg and followed him. At the exit to Scotland Yard's forbidding precincts they parted company . . . and met again the following morning at nine, to find that nothing exciting had happened during the night. There was the information that an inquest would be held on Janice Mottram the following day, and the men watching Mary Lilian Street had reported that no unusual event had transpired. A relief group of men had now taken over.

'Which all seems very tame after the fun we've been having,' Hancock commented, hanging up his hat and then rubbing his scalp. 'Well, just a matter of sitting waiting, I suppose . . . Meantime I'd better get my own notes on the business written up. If there isn't some action soon I'll make an arrest anyway

— but I'd have much preferred that she walk into the trap herself . . . '

He settled in his swivel chair and drew some foolscap towards him to commence writing; then he glanced up as a constable brought in a cablegram and laid it down on the desk.

'Thanks,' Hancock said genially. 'Grand morning, Bert — Bring on the seeds like — I'll be thrice damned!' Hancock finished staring at the cable.

The constable went out silently. Grimshaw came over to the desk quickly.

'Something wrong, sir?'

'I'll say there is! Look at this — 'Whittaker family you mention all killed in tenement fire in January, 1944. Positively verified. Chief of Police, Cape Town, South Africa'.'

The sergeant frowned. 'Say, that rather alters matters, doesn't it? You've worked it out that Sybil Whittaker was the killer. She can't be if she died in a fire, can she?'

'This must he wrong,' Hancock growled, staring at the cable. 'It must be, if it isn't then my whole reasoning falls to bits from top to bottom!' He sat for a while meditating, then he relaxed and gave a woeful grin. 'Just shows you it doesn't do to go putting the finger on people until you're sure. I may have been wrong all along the line. If so it means I'll have to start all over again — a prospect which makes me weep!'

'How do you start to check whether you're right or wrong, sir?' Grimshaw asked.

'All I can do is wait and see if anything happens in Mary Lilian Street, and if it doesn't I . . . ' Hancock stopped and shrugged his heavy shoulders.

'I just don't know,' he confessed moodily. 'I'll have no idea where to look because nothing will fit into place. Something must happen in Mary Lilian Street finally!' he insisted. 'It's got to! It's the goal the killer has been striving to reach from the very start!'

Disgruntled, he turned back to making his notes, and indeed he remained at them, with breaks for meals, for the greater part of the day. That he was deeply impatient and doing his best to control it, Grimshaw knew full well. He said nothing, however, when his superior was in this kind of mood anything was likely to happen. Hancock could be just as unpleasant sometimes as normally he was genial.

It was nearing eight-thirty, with the night setting in, when he gave vent to his feeling. Tossing down his extinguished pipe on the desk, he got on his feet and paced back and forth across the drab little office, pausing ever and again to glare through the window at the twinkling lights on the Embankment.

'South Africa must be wrong,' he kept insisting. 'They've got to be! They've got their facts mixed up somewhere! I tell you, Harry, that I — ' He swung to the door at a knock. 'Yes, come in,' he growled.

A plain-clothes man entered and advanced to the desk.

'We caught a woman in Mary Lilian Street, sir,' he said briefly. 'So, according to your orders, we brought her over straight away.'

'Ah!' A gleam came into Hancock's pale eyes. His expression was instantly changed to something bordering on good humor. 'It worked, then! Splendid! Bring her in.'

Shadows moved in the corridor outside, then a second plain-clothes man entered, holding a woman by the arm. She came into the full area of the single electric light hanging over the desk, and stared fixedly at Hancock. He gazed back.

'I thought I was right,' he said quietly, and in his own corner Sergeant Grimshaw looked at the woman's tall, graceful young figure and neat two-piece. He frowned, not recognizing her. She had fair hair that tumbled prettily to her shoulders, and was not wearing a hat. Her slim hands, strong in the way she clenched the edge of the desk, were nonetheless white and feminine.

'All right, boys,' Hancock said, jerking his head. 'Thanks.'

The two p.c. men went out. Hancock motioned.

'Sit down, Betty, won't you?' he invited quietly. And to Grimshaw he added, 'This is Mrs. Cavendish, Harry — Tom Cavendish's wife.'

Betty Cavendish sat down very slowly, her keen gray eyes fixed on the Chief Inspector's face. The wide mouth, which had smiled and laughed so infectiously when he had visited the Cavendish home for an evening was now set in a thin, bitter line.

'Don't imagine I'm enjoying this, Betty,' Hancock said seriously, reaching down to his pipe and picking it up. 'I haven't enjoyed one moment of this case since I got the first suspicion that it was you I was looking for. You're the wife of one of my best friends. It makes it tough — for him and for me.'

Betty Cavendish relaxed a little and the hard line of her mouth broke into a cynical smile. It was a surprising revelation to Hancock, recalling to mind the carefree manner she had had on the night of his visit.

'You don't suppose that your plain-clothes men picking me up in Mary Lilian Street means anything, do you?' she asked dryly.

'I am inclined to think it means everything,' Hancock told her, digging out his pipe bowl with a penknife. 'They had orders only to pick up any woman who searched Mary Lilian Street. That is what you must have been doing, otherwise they would not have picked you up. I would say that you were searching for diamonds to the approximate tune of a hundred thousand pounds.'

'Absurd!' Betty snapped. 'After all, Billy — I can still call you Billy, I suppose?' she broke off.

'If it makes you any happier. I shall do my job no matter what you call me.'

'All right, then; it's absurd. I wasn't searching for anything. I was just looking around.'

'Why?'

'Well, I'm new in this country, am I not? What could be more natural?'

'I could understand it better if it were not night,' Hancock said, and tipped a little heap of ash in the brass tray. Then he added, 'Why try wrapping things up, Sybil? I know all about you — to the tiniest detail. That's my job, you know.'

She started very slightly at the mention

of the name. A touch of heightened color came into her smooth cheeks.

'My name isn't Sybil, it's Betty! Formerly Betty Dyson, and now Betty Cavendish.'

'Originally Sybil Whittaker, daughter of James and Mildred Whittaker, of Vildon Street, East London. For something like thirteen years you lived in the same house with the three Bradmore sisters. Finally there came a time when you and your parents went to Cape Town and the three Bradmore sisters set off into the world on their own.'

The girl stared blankly, neither troubling to confirm or deny the statement. Hancock filled his pipe bowl carefully, lighted it, then sat in the swivel chair. There was no anger in his round face. Instead he looked like a father about to scold an aberrant daughter.

'My guess,' he said, 'is that you went from South Africa to America when you were in the region of twenty. There you changed your name to Betty Dyson. In that name, you won various sports — as witness those cups you proudly showed me. It dawned on me then that you were the athletic type — the sort with strong physique, who might climb up to a fourth floor window.'

Betty Cavendish sank back a little in her chair. Whatever emotion she was experiencing was revealed in the way she played with the gloves in her lap. Hancock eased forward a little in his chair, watching her face intently.

'When you took over your pseudonym and struck out in America I believe you did it with only one aim — to find as quickly as possible a man whom you could marry, an Englishman, who would bring you back to England with him. I also believe your aim was to shelter behind a respectable name. That chance came when Tom Cavendish met you. You married him — and came back to this country with only one intention . . . to find the Bradmore sisters and piece together the tattoos on their backs.'

'I like your imagination, Billy,' the girl said coolly. 'For that's what it is, you know. You can't prove a word of it!'

Hancock was undeterred. 'Your father

and mother died in a tenement fire in South Africa. I've proved that. But you escaped. I have proved that too — '

'But you couldn't have . . . ' Betty stopped herself, a glint in her eyes. 'I mean I . . . '

'You died in the fire?' Hancock suggested calmly.

Caught by the subtle trickery of his question, she glared at him bitterly.

'All right, so I am Sybil Whittaker,' she snapped. 'You've proved that much, it seems, so I may as well admit it. No crime in doing so. I didn't die in that fire, though. A friend called on the evening it happened. Similar to me in build. Nobody knew she called except my mother and father. When the building went up in flames I managed to escape. I guessed my friend's remains would be taken to be mine — and later I read they were. Then I assumed my new identity and made my way to America. I'd have come to England there and then only the war was on and things were difficult. I didn't fancy bombing, so . . . ' she shrugged.

'I think,' Hancock said, 'that somewhere you heard your father mention that a hundred thousand in gems was lying waiting to be picked up, if only he knew where. By snatches and drifts I think you gathered that he had once been involved in a diamond robbery. You then remembered the triplets with whom you had spent your earlier life — children of the diamond robber — and your shrewd mind pieced together the meaning of the tattoos, only you probably couldn't then remember them.'

'Yes,' Betty whispered, lowering her gaze. 'Yes — that's right. But I don't see why I should sit here and admit it!'

'I'll tell you this much, Betty — if you don't admit it, the Court will so hammer home every fact before it's finished that you'll have to. Whatever extenuating circumstances there may be in this case — and God knows I can't see any — they'll be given more consideration if you make a full confession.'

The girl was silent for a long time, then she hunched one shoulder and lowered it again.

'All right. I knew I was taking a frightful risk, and I knew the penalty. I just lost my gamble, that's all. I'll tell you everything.'

Hancock got to his feet. 'Before you do I'm officially charging you with the murder of Vera Bradmore, Elsie Jackson, and Janice Mottram, and I have to warn you that — '

'All right, all right, I know all about that stuff!' Betty interrupted curtly. Then for a moment she sat thinking, evidently getting her thoughts into order. Grimshaw, at his desk, sat with his hand poised over his notebook in readiness, pencil in his fingers.

'You seemed to have guessed most of it, Billy,' Betty said finally. 'As you say, I did live with the three Bradmore girls during my early life — or rather they lived with me. I shared the same bedroom with them. Naturally, I wondered quite a lot about those tattoos, but being young I didn't give them overmuch thought.

'It was not until father, mother, and I were domiciled in Cape Town that I had reason to think of them again. One evening, when we had a kind of family conference to decide how to make our money spin out, my father said it was galling to be without much cash when some hundred thousand pounds' worth of diamonds were lying somewhere in London, if he only knew where. He openly admitted that that he had been mixed up in the diamond robbery. So many years had passed he didn't see much harm in confessing the fact to Mother and me . . . The upshot was that he couldn't understand why Arthur Bradmore had never tipped him off as to where the diamonds were. I found out by degrees that neither my father nor my mother had ever attached importance to the tattoos. Knowing Arthur Bradmore was a tattooist, they had assumed, I think, that he had been conducting some sort of experiment on his children. But I thought further, and it finally dawned on me that had Arthur Bradmore wanted to send a message without attracting the attention of the police, that might be the only way he could do it — '

Betty broke off suddenly, seized by an unexpected fit of coughing. She finished up with her eyes watering. From a flat lozenge tin in her bag, she took a cough drop and sucked it.

'This confounded climate,' she said bitterly. 'Er — I made up my mind to get back to England and have another look at the tattoos — which I couldn't possibly remember. You know how I did that. My chance came when I apparently died in the fire; that gave me the opportunity to take on a new identity altogether and so, I hoped, give me freedom of movement. Back I came to England and found Vera Bradmore. From her I learned where the other sisters were. If Vera had changed her name, like her sisters, I would probably never have succeeded in my efforts. My biggest shock came when I learned that Tom was a friend of yours, and that you were actively engaged on the case. I insisted on him bringing you to meet me. I wanted to sum up the opposition. Even when I had the three names — 'Mary — Lil — Ian' — it took me some time to realize what they implied. I worked it out finally from a map of London when it occurred to me it might mean a particular street. Tonight I decided to risk looking for the diamonds in that street — and was immediately picked up.'

Betty stopped talking and coughed harshly again. The attack took some time to subside. Hancock's pipe crackled as he sat studying her.

'More or less as I'd worked it out — with one or two omissions on your part,' he said. 'I'll clear those up right now . . . Firstly, it was ego on your part that led you to ask Tom to bring me to see you. You wanted to have that supreme advantage beloved of all criminals — the chance to laugh at the man trying to track you down. However, I learned far more than you imagined. Apart from the cups on the mantle — which told me of your athletic prowess — I also noticed the number of crime books you had, and indeed to which you drew my attention. From those you had possibly learned many 'tricks of the trade.' I also noticed your slightly nasal accent. When you told me you were London born, I began to think things . . . '

Hancock took his pipe from his teeth and considered it.

'Later, when I questioned the maid Ella, she told me that a woman visitor who had enquired about the beach cottage had had a slightly American twang in her voice. This further verified my suspicion that it was you I was looking for. I suggest that you first rang up the Jacksons to find out what moves you could make. You learned they were at the cottage and went there — killing Elsie Jackson whilst her husband slept. You then came back post haste to London and, adding a dark wig and glasses, presented yourself at the Jackson home to say your business was not so important after all. Reason? You hoped that way to show you had never left town, and also your vanity tempted you into providing what you thought would be an alibi if suspicion ever rested on you. You'd have done better not to have acted that way. Your voice, which you effectually disguised over the telephone, gave you away when you met Ella face to face.'

Betty was silent, the color gone from her cheeks. She was looking curiously sleepy. Hancock gave a grim smile:

'At first I suspected Tom,' he said. 'Chiefly because he was away at the times of the murders; then it occurred to me, once I had checked his movements and found them okay, that whilst he was away you had freedom of movement. You could do as you chose without him knowing anything about it . . . I admit you were clever in some things, Betty, but not clever enough.'

Betty was still silent. For a moment, she licked her lips slowly and a spasm seemed to contort her face. Hancock gazed at her fixedly for a second or two and then leapt to his feet. As he did so, the girl reeled sideways out of her chair and slumped heavily to the office floor. Almost immediately Hancock was kneeling beside her, raising her eyelids from dulled pupils.

'Poison,' he said briefly. 'Quick, Harry — get Doc Fisher! Must have been that damned lozenge she took.'

Grimshaw jumped to the door and out into the passageway. Hancock raised the girl's head and shoulders in his right arm, and for a moment consciousness came back to her.

'Don't — waste your time, Billy,' she whispered. 'I knew — I'd have to do this — if things went wrong. In that lozenge — there was — half a grain of atropine. That's a fatal dose. I read it — in a book on poisons . . . '

She relapsed again, breathing shallowly. Within a few moments Dr. Fisher had arrived. He kneeled down quickly at the girl's side and took her wrist. After a second or two he looked up.

'No use, Billy,' he said, shrugging. 'She's dead . . . I'll have to find out what she took.'

'It was atropine,' Hancock said, and from the handbag on the table he handed over the box of lozenges. 'She said half a grain, but I imagine it must have been more — '

'Not necessarily.' The doctor stood up. 'Half a grain is fatal — and quick-acting. Well, I'll send in two boys with a stretcher and have the body put in my surgery for the time being until your report's complete.'

Fisher went out again, and Hancock

met the eyes of the sergeant over the girl's body.

'Evidently she was no more afraid to die, sir, than she was to commit murder. Going to be tough for you, breaking the news to Mr. Cavendish.'

'Damned tough,' the Chief Inspector muttered. 'And all so blasted useless, too!'

'Useless, sir?'

'Certainly! No need for any of it! Mary Lilian Street, as it was in the days when Arthur Bradmore hid the diamonds somewhere in it is no more. The blitz destroyed it and all the surrounding property. The present Mary Lilian Street is a narrow kind of alleyway, but she could not know that. I checked up on that when I went to look at the street the other night. I remembered that dock area had been heavily bombed so I investigated . . . Somewhere in the dust and ruins that underlie the new street are the remains of those diamonds . . . '

Hancock stopped and sighed. 'It makes you think,' he muttered. 'It really does.'

We do hope that you have enjoyed reading this large print book.

Did you know that all of our titles are available for purchase?

We publish a wide range of high quality large print books including:
Romances, Mysteries, Classics
General Fiction
Non Fiction and Westerns

Special interest titles available in large print are:
The Little Oxford Dictionary
Music Book, Song Book
Hymn Book, Service Book

Also available from us courtesy of Oxford University Press:
Young Readers' Dictionary
(large print edition)
Young Readers' Thesaurus
(large print edition)

For further information or a free brochure, please contact us at:
Ulverscroft Large Print Books Ltd.,
The Green, Bradgate Road, Anstey,
Leicester, LE7 7FU, England.
Tel: (00 44) **0116 236 4325**
Fax: (00 44) **0116 234 0205**

Other titles in the
Linford Mystery Library:

DEATH CALLED AT NIGHT

R. A. Bennett

Jimmy Ellis believes his parents have died in a car crash when as a young boy he is taken to live with relatives in Australia. The years pass happily, then the nightmare comes. Terrifying images flit through his mind in the dark — all through the eyes of a child, a witness to grisly events seventeen years before. He begins to delve into the past, and soon he finds himself on the trail of a double murderer — a murderer who is prepared to kill again.